brok

broken news

amrita tripathi

TRANQUEBAR

TRANQUEBAR PRESS
An imprint of westland ltd
Venkat Towers, 165, P.H. Road, Opp. Maduravoyal Municipal Office, Chennai 600 095
No.38/10 (New No.5), Raghava Nagar, New Timber Yard Layout, Bangalore 560 026
Survey No. A-9, II Floor, Moula Ali Industrial Area, Moula Ali, Hyderabad 500 040
Plot No 102, Marol Coop Ind Estate, Marol, Andheri East, Mumbai 400 059
47, Brij Mohan Road, Daryaganj, New Delhi 110 002

First published in India by TRANQUEBAR PRESS 2010

Copyright © Amrita Tripathi 2010

All rights reserved

10 9 8 7 6 5 4 3 2 1

ISBN: 978-93-80032-67-2

Typeset in Weiss Roman by SÜRYA, New Delhi
Printed at Thomson Press, New Delhi

This book is sold subject to the condition that it shall not by way of trade or otherwise, be lent, resold, hired out, circulated, and no reproduction in any form, in whole or in part (except for brief quotations in critical articles or reviews) may be made without written permission of the publishers.

γνῶθι σεαυτόν

Contents

Prologue: The Space Between		ix
PART 1: PRE-BREAKDOWN		
1.	Disowning the Gods	5
2.	Life Lessons: Easier Taught than Learned	13
3.	It Gets Personal	31
4.	Hairline Cracks and the Rhythm	47
5.	Whining, Bitching, Back-biting	73
6.	Redemption Song	89
7.	From the Sidelines	103
8.	Inner Steel and Icy Disappointment	113
9.	Emergency Dash Autopilot	125
	Interlude: Blackout	134
PART 2: POST-BREAKDOWN		
1.	Papering the Cracks	139
2.	Surviving Death	149
3.	Planning His Downfall	161

VIII CONTENTS

4.	Day of Mourning	173
5.	Shrink-wrapped	183
6.	Raking in the Karma	195
7.	Shattering the Calm	211
8.	Exit Point	221
	Epilogue	233
	Acknowledgements	235

Prologue: The Space Between

I'm not going to tell you my name just yet. Call me M. That'll do for now. You'll find that annoying, I know, right here at the outset, but you'll get why, by and by. It's really just a tiny precaution I'm taking, you know, just because it would not do at all, it would spoil *everything*, if you knew who I really was.

I mean, let's face it, I've been around a while, you've probably seen me on TV, you might already know me, and that just automatically means you'll come in with all these pre-conceptions. And that wouldn't do at all.

Trust me on this one.

The rest is all fine, believe me. You'll know it, intuitively. Real stories. Real people. Real shit hitting the fan. Real names, more importantly.

Oh, except Susheel. I'm not going to tell you his real name either. All things considered, I'm safer off that way. Suffice it to say, no matter what everyone thinks, he's still a menace.

I'm convinced it's fraying — the boundaries are fraying, between this, your / their world and mine. Their reality and mine. The would-be / could-be / didn't quite-happen but did. And yet no one else sees it quite the same way.

X PROLOGUE

At least that's how it seemed to go down. That's the bitch about perspective.

In the end, though, let's face it, we all cave. The little people, we don't have much of a say in our reality.

So yeah, I see it all fraying. Well, go on then, before it's all gone, *fwoosh*, get in.

Part 1

PRE-BREAKDOWN

1. Disowning the Gods

'Myself Janki,' she told me, this slip of a girl. Completely overshadowed by the super-confident bunch from the Asian College of Journalism. It was touching really—well, almost. Everyone's here to be a star, after all. Which can get to be a drag, when you've been around as long as I have . . . eight years in TV, still going strong (with a dash of cynicism thrown in).

'Myself media professional. Myself insignificant,' I finished up for her, or wait, that was just a thought bubble. How many times have we cringed with this sort of conversation, in our superior English-educated skins.

Maybe because of all those times, my heart went out to her. We'll make her a star yet, I told myself, eager to embark on a new project—because, let's face it, sometimes a lot of what we do here in this TV empire is ultimately too fleeting to be significant.

At least, that's the way I've started feeling. It's years since I've been 'established', I suppose you would call it, and I've been in this strange cocoon for a while now—I've lost a bit of my drive, just in the face of all the crap I see. We're running around so fast in circles, it's like gerbils on a treadmill—it makes you lose perspective.

6 BROKEN NEWS

But giving someone a boost, watching them fill out their space, project a sense of authority—well, that would be something else altogether. The bigger the challenge, the better at this point, I'm thinking.

And after that trip to Jaipur—tourist paradise and oh-so-lovely setting of a literary festival—I'm beginning to think there's not much that's different between us. Sure, my friends and I bring a more refined version of this kid to the table, but we're all Janki-esque, if you will ... there's always someone we're looking to impress. Like the phirangs we were sitting with. We slipped into post-colonial mode without a thought.

They lead, we follow. An ageing blonde hippie, her more sullen partner facing off from the two of us, Indian kids lost for cover, looking for a little space to claim. Which we don't ... not here, at this lavish party, thrown for grand guests traipsing into the unknown. Except it is so known, so done to death. Is there a bigger cliché than Jaipur and Rajasthan, the forts and deserts, and colour and ... a conversation jolts me out of my self-indulgent reverie. Surrounded by clichés.

The power couple have brought in their friends. They mingle for a bit, do the local flavour, and then retire to the lavish by-invite-only farm parties—all dressed the part in ethnic chic, swaying to the fusion music that pounds out, into space. Ageing gently in the desert sun, listening to people introduce themselves as *Man*ish and Pra*modh*— the emphasis in all the wrong places as we look to impress.

'What does your name mean?' asks the sixty-year-old freckled, tank-top-wearing aunty, Evelyn, except she's not an aunty at all. I mean, she's white, for one. And then there's the fact that she acted in soaps back in LA.

She's moved on now—found herself, courtesy her guru. 'He's up near the Beas,' she tells us, smiling indulgently, as if to say everyone should have their own personal guru. Whatever. We're all sold out here, I feel like saying, twentieth-century India's moved way beyond; we want our malls and capitalist gods, not self-help and salvation, thank you very much.

She's undeterred—maybe because none of this is said aloud. Her guru is the best, she lets us know, and she's introduced him to her ex-biker friend, who looks mildly drunk. He tosses a few suspicious glances over at us. He wants to get where it's at, and sitting around the little bonfire doesn't seem like his scene at all.

Stories of liberation and enlightenment wash over me— rather pleasantly, I think—but she takes me for a sceptic, because I'm not contributing any of my own. That's surely part of the deal, she indicates. I mean, she is talking about *my* religion *my* culture, and here I am, disowning it with an ever-so-slight smirk.

I don't mean to sound pretentious or condescending at all, but I can't possibly take all this crap seriously, I mean, really. I try and smile benignly, hopefully conveying a greater spiritual connect—I mean, that *is* my cultural legacy, after all.

What actually comes across, I have no doubt, is somewhat more obnoxious.

'What's your name . . . what does it mean? I love the way Indian names always mean something,' she tells us, adding that she wants to change her name Evelyn to something more exciting.

8 BROKEN NEWS

'My name?' I say, and shrug. I have no intentions of explaining the etymology of M. But my friend Nandini now, she's up for the game.

'Bountiful cow,' she says.

'What!'

'Yes, exactly that,' Nandini continues. 'My parents named me bountiful cow.' She gets more than her fair share of laughs. I'm in splits too, actually.

'You don't believe in any of this?' Evelyn asks me, pointedly.

'Any of what?'

'Deeper meanings, god, your religion, what your name means, what you symbolise in the cosmos?' She's not letting me get away that easily, is Evelyn. I start to tell her, I've always wanted a middle name actually, Suzanne, maybe, but I keep it simple.

'Well,' I say, 'no, I have no issues with my name. But if we're talking religion, well, erm, that is to say, I'm Hindu, but non-practising.'

Oh, how our gods are looking down, losing face as we speak. Disinherited, just like that, over a cold beer. If only they could regain those lost powers and strike us down, smite us. Not for blasphemy, but for being a bunch of pussies. Not defending their honour, not re-claiming them out of the exotica.

But Evelyn's clearly touched a nerve with me, killing my buzz. 'Fuck you and fuck your guru,' I get up to leave. 'Leave me and my fucking religion out of this.'

Except, of course, this is all in my head: I'm much too well brought-up for that. Well brought-up, well-meaning, left of centre and an armchair liberal . . . you know the type. Hell, you probably *are* the type.

PRE-BREAKDOWN 9

As I try and turn away, I spy with my little eye, Ish—except he says it EEsh. A twenty-one-year-old hottie who makes 'doccos' on travelling in India—for an international channel, he's quick to point out.

'Can I join you guys,' he asks Evelyn, then quickly includes Nandini and me.

'What a pseudo!' I rip him apart in my racially-charged mind—but I'm the one going for the easy laugh now, with the mock-Indian accent I put on, imitating a colleague. Funny how I'm willing to betray my heritage—for youth, for beauty, acceptance, a quick lay. Funny how I see he's Brit, but the bountiful cow sees the Indian in him.

'So you're from around here?' asks Nandini, after he's done chatting Evelyn up.

'Oh no, I'm not. I'm Brit to the bone, actually,' he says. She doesn't look convinced. 'My family's Poon-jabi,' he adds. And that really does sum it up. Cheers, mate.

'The party, let's go,' he's saying. I know it's cradle-snatching—what am I thinking! But no, Nandini's not going, and though I really want to, I'm not quite willing to exit my comfort zone. And there is the almost-real thing I have going back home. Fuck this, let's get dinner at the hotel and crash early, I tell her.

Heritage and conservative norms intact.

2. Life Lessons:
Easier Taught than Learned

So when I meet Janki, the brown girl in the ring, Indian to the core and with none of the identity issues my gang and I suffer from—none that I can tell straight off, anyway—well, I figure *here's* a project to shake off the boredom.

I know she's looking to re-invent herself. You can tell immediately, with the trying-too-hard clothes, so last-season, and the hair and make-up done just so.

Wow, I've really grown into this role of mentor, I think to myself. Why, just the other day, a young intern (now all grown-up, and finishing her diploma course at IIMC) called me for advice. Career advice, no less. Imagine that! Of course, it's the whole package they're buying into, I know that: my ego isn't a size that blocks out reality—not yet anyway.

In fact, I'm pretty sure Janki just came up to me because I'm in full battle gear: blazer and spaghetti, make-up and hair still in place, fully accessorised, sitting around after a bulletin, waiting for that adrenaline rush to die down, an hour-and-a-half to go till the next show.

14 BROKEN NEWS

'Send me an email and resumé,' I'd trilled into the phone to my former intern. And acquitted myself rather well, I thought, with some generalities on what to expect in this big, ever-expanding glitter-ation that is the media, tempered with some caution: 'You understand the economic slowdown's hit the industry in a big way; there's a freeze on hiring all over. But I'll see what I can do.'

Janki forces herself into my mind space with her jabbering. 'I live close to the office,' she tells me, 'like you.' I raise an eyebrow: she knows where I live and acts like it's an instant bond that we both live in east Delhi. In Mayur Vihar, a stone's throw from our Noida office . . . A suburb that's captured the essence of the Indian middle class so deeply, so thoroughly, that it's turned grey. And it's not just the buildings: the dreams, the air, everything is thick with it. Oh, the dull self-effacement of it; the quiet overwhelming industriousness of it. No glamour here, that's for sure.

In TV terms, we're not People Like Us, or PLUs, (used to define people we focus on in our shoots, people our audience will connect with instantly). Not for us (for the most part) the struggling rickshaw-wallah and his wife and nine-year-old who get more play on international TV than they do on our channels. International audiences lap it up, but not ours, I'm told. Hey, I don't make the rules, what do I know! I'm not even our target audience, judging by my postal code.

But you can't define me by where I live: I'm here on rent, and that's only because office is some three kilometres away, I'm quick to point out to anyone who'll listen.

And I'm not grey.

PRE-BREAKDOWN 15

And in any case *my* apartment block is not really grey: it's a fetching mélange of brickwork and shit-pipes, green park and pigeon shit (they're grey, it's greenish), dust and lizards. Delightful, really. So, as I take pains to point out, I'm like you that way: obsessed with class if not caste, postal code if not integrity, and definitely—definitely— bank balance, if not career options.

That's me, Delhi to the core. Loud and brash and aggressive, on the one hand, but also courteous and old-world . . . and yet ambitious like all the young blood in this city—ultimately, utterly, butterly pseudo.

To the core.

But Janki now, to me, she's fresh: twenty-one, just out of a media course that she fought her ageing, conservative parents to attend, she tells me. They wanted her to take the Civils, which is of course the deepest desire of parents of a certain generation. The images they hold close to their hearts are of lal-batti Ambassadors, their kids wielding absolute power in some god-forsaken district in some god-forsaken corner of the country. But you have to be of, well, a certain bent of mind, I suppose, to want to live that dream.

Janki tells me she'd spent the better part of her last year of college trying to prepare simultaneously for end-of-year exams as well as the Civils. She hadn't done very well in either. Her friends were still holed up in Mukherjee Nagar slogging it out, she said. Hell, I wouldn't be surprised if some of *my* friends were still there from eight years ago, swotting away, hoping that this is the year they crack the whole thing.

But Janki forces me back to her. 'The classes were just

too much,' she shakes her head ruefully. It was a tough fight, but she has a year's reprieve from her parents to prove herself, she tells me. And she's charged up—that, she doesn't have to tell me. It oozes out of her, not pushy or aggressive, so much as endearing, in a way. No south Delhi dreams for her. No blushing away the question, 'Where do you live?' Bounded by a river and the greyness of the air, she's not choked by it, like I am.

And for this, I like her.

'That's great, I'm sure you'll be great,' I say, trying not to be intimidating. Because that really does go with the territory—with Anchordom. It can be a lot to digest.

You're on TV, it changes you. Sure, it's insidious at first and you barely notice, but there's no denying it after a point. Face the camera more than a handful of times, and you're a poser for life. I mean, you're talking, you're frikkin' emoting and smiling at something inanimate! You're told to act as if it's 'someone in their living room', but are you kidding me? You gotta be a head case to make this work. And no, the camera person doesn't count—he's not listening to you, anyway!

But it goes beyond that. Being on TV changes the way people react to you: there's a larger-than-life aura around you now, something familiar and yet inaccessible . . . Suddenly people are happy to know you, even if it's a hi-hello sort of knowing—something about the glamour seeps out, off-screen. So when you look *through* people, it doesn't bother them, that's what they expect. If you do acknowledge them, it's a bonus. Not your office colleagues so much, of course, because they know the pre-TV you, and the off-screen you, and anyway they don't think you're any great shit—if they'd been at the right place at the right time, well, *you'd* be fluttering around *them*. And btw, that's not entirely untrue either.

But there are fewer of my peers around here now, practically ten years down the line. A lot of them have moved, switched jobs, switched channels, looking to build their own brand equity, getting fatter and fatter pay packets.

But just by sticking around this long, I'm becoming one of what we used to call 'the holy cows', back when we were younger. No one's really going to fuck with me, at this point, and you know what? No one should. I've really put my blood and sweat and guts into helping build this empire, not to mention my youth. All of my twenties, practically. And it's time to reap the dividends. Not that you can sit your ass down and get comfy for too long, there's always a group of people breathing down your neck, thinking they can do better than you, more than you, outshine you! But yeah, we wear our time here like a badge: it's become something we have in common, a shield against the Lesser-Known, the fresh recruits.

Honestly, I can't even tell you whether this is really my first conversation with Janki. She's probably smiled at me, or greeted me reverentially before, for all I know. Hell, I might even have smiled back. I'm nothing if not quick with that breezy, fake smile—I flash it at pretty much everyone I know. What can I say, there's only so much posing you can do before it becomes a part of who you are. Just don't let your friends see you at it. There's nothing more infuriating, I've been told.

They don't take my bullshit, my friends. I have a great

18 BROKEN NEWS

core group. Or at least I did, till the big break-up last year. There's another wake-up call for you. But at least now I know there are two who'll see me through anything. Ankita and Karthik, I can always fall back on. I've been there for them too, now, don't get me wrong but well . . . not as much of late as I should have, I guess. The one thing this job doesn't leave you with, is much time. I think we signed a contract somewhere—'thou shalt not have a life outside work'. It makes it difficult, to keep friendships, relationships going. But I don't want to dump this on Janki just yet. Or even bring up the bitchy rivalries, with even your best friends! It's so high school, in a way.

Over the years, with our career paths constantly clashing, I've become slightly alienated from three of my at-one-time-closest friends. We're always secretly watching to see who's getting bigger or getting more airtime, whose shows are getting the TRPs. Oh, the ratings game: we all disown it, but secretly crave mass approval. I don't even get how they come up with ratings—but I do notice who gets recognised on the streets more (me: twice in one session, Preeti by *four* people! She's obviously no longer my favourite TV friend! But, really, who wants to host a cooking show anyway, right?).

Besides Preeti, there's Jenny, the gorgeous girl with her own show at the age of twenty-four. I almost died of jealousy at the time. Well, neither of us is twenty-four any more, but the competition was really between her and me, a few years ago. All part of the game—and then I blew them both out of the water, getting into news, and nearing prime-time, and even better, getting my own special weekend show. I got to travel and do a youth-speaks sort of show that had great ratings, great sponsorship, and it was high profile—so it was win-win. As in, I win.

Okay, fine, so I like winning as much as the next guy, don't you go judging me. I'm building my own life, my own following, brick by fucking brick. And taking the falls too, in my own time.

'There's so much I can teach you,' I feel like saying to Janki, as I wait for her to gather the courage to come out with it, what she's bursting to say—that she wants to be on air, that she wants to be part of urban history in the making, however fleeting that is. That she wants the glamour of it all.

And trust me, once it's in your blood, it's there for good. No one walks out on that. Unless you don't make it all the way, of course—but then, that's a whole new ball game. Look at Preeti's older sister, Priya. She was part of that golden generation of Indian TV journos, at the centre of it all when it really kicked off in the '90s: English news the way the country had never seen it before. Priya was a part of that sacred space, the TV empire that just kept growing: we saw her everywhere.

We were in college, lapping it all up and unabashedly loved her. She was my hero. The Christiane Amanpour mould I was hoping to grow into. And then, all of a sudden, she was nowhere. She quit. I'm not entirely sure what happened, but whispers on the grapevine even back in college were of a burnout. And some shady, shadowy producer-figure in the background. Preeti would clamp up whenever I'd ask her and I never heard anything substantial about her again, even after I joined TV.

20 BROKEN NEWS

I learned the lesson. Once you're out of TV, no one cares anymore, you mean nothing, you're just not significant. The Fallen-by-the-Waysiders: who knows where they end up.

Well, times are changing—now, for one thing, there's no lack of choice . . . thirty-eight-and-some news channels, though the big fight's between the top three or four, naturally. But even if news isn't your thing, I'm told there are now more than three hundred cable and satellite and terrestrial channels, so the entire country's your oyster. This is the El Dorado of our times after all, but who knows what a shake-down in a couple of years will bring.

There's also the magazine route many gravitate towards, when the insane pressure and eighteen-hour days finally get too much. Or you could switch over to the other side altogether, like some of my slightly more annoying friends have done: join PR.

Back to me for the moment. Because I don't have to worry about fading away, I've still got it. I worked my ass off to get here, and I'm not going anywhere in a frikkin' hurry. That came out all defensive, I know, but anchoring apart, I think I've hit a bit of a dry patch. After all, you're only as good as your last show, your last story, and to keep pumping out quality stuff takes some staying power. I need some good ideas, and fast. Somehow, of late, they've been drying up in my head.

I've been doing the news anchoring and that youth show I was telling you about, but I need to recharge. And keep reminding myself I've still got game. Around here, they know it. Which is why I've finally got some regular promos on air now—you know, those short clips featuring hotshot anchors and reporters. The proof you're looking for, that I certainly have made my way maybe three-quarters up that goddamn ladder.

Janki's trying to tell me she saw, and liked, my women's health special. That reminds me, it's a show I did last year, which was just nominated for a national TV award. Not too shabby!

What's funny though is you're always looking around to see who's doing what, better! Despite what you see and hear of the star tantrums, everyone's a tad insecure. You've got to be, to stay in the game. Healthy self-esteem is something you rarely see around here. And why I'm on edge now, is I feel I have to prove myself all over again. Well, I'm not sure. Some of it may just be in my own head. The last couple of months have cast a bit of a pall over everything, with my personal life intruding into my professional, which is always ugly. That's what I have to sort of rub out of public memory now. I feel my frown lines etching themselves into permanence. And one two three . . . unfurrow. Aaaand release.

Back to the moment.

'I wanted your help. There's a story I want to do . . . Can I sit?' Janki's voice is taking on an insistent tone.

She's kind of in my space now, a little bit, towering over me as I stare into my computer. I minimise the window; it really annoys me when people peep into my screen, as they so often do when they come up to chat—like she's doing right now. Not that there's much space for her to manoeuvre—our computers are barely three feet apart, and my next-door neighbour Chandrika here, the grump, is firmly wedged into her seat.

'Sure, what's it on?' You can't tell from my tone at all, but really, I'm not this patient. I feel like saying: I've gone down this road with millions of other people . . . interns, deskies, anyone who feels the burning urge to be in front of the camera. It's only ever meant anything when they're as passionate about telling a story. But let's face it, most everyone just wants to see themselves on TV. Not even the most reticent producers can deny that sneaking urge at some much-hidden level. I'm all for it. I mean, I'm not saying just because I've been doing this for eight years, I deserve to be on air any more than you, or some young twenty-one-year-old chit of a girl. Even a lunk from the Stone Age could do a better job than some of the puffed egos running this joint.

At least that's my jaded thought bubble, breaking into the conversation. *Of course you can. It's not rocket science. You get an idea, think it through, go out, execute, come back, and we'll slap it on air.* I don't actually say this, of course. I wish I could, but it would just be rude on too many levels.

'It's on uterine infections,' Janki tells me. I'm aghast. Jaw to floor.

'What!'

'Three of my friends have just got UTI in the past month, and no one really knows what to do about it—or even what it is, really. I want to do a story.'

I'm nothing if not a hypochondriac, so I'm all of a sudden wondering if I've been feeling that slightly burning sensation when I go . . . no, no, thank god. That was a couple of years ago, when I almost died of a UTI, courtesy a very misguided one-night stand. Oh, youth!

But then again, what the hell does this girl think she's

going to shoot? 'Hmm, what do you plan to shoot?' And more importantly, who have her friends been sleeping with, without protection! But again, not the politest question to ask.

'I don't know. Will you help me?' she says.

Me! I don't have time to pee around here, half the time.

'No, I will not,' I start to say, but then remember my whole mental conversation, the comma in the air, the fact that she might need real guidance, and that I, M, might now firmly be in Guide-Mentor mode.

'Fine, yes, send me an email and we'll figure it out,' I hear myself saying.

Send me an email: the closest thing to a nail in the coffin. Designed for PR types who keep jabbering away in your ear—calling and messaging, and calling again on landline, cellphone, landline . . . and you've got no other way of dealing with it. Until they take it upon themselves to land up at your office. Send me a mail, we tell them. Send me a mail because I'm too busy to remember and process what you've just finished telling me. Because I'm important and you're not. Send me a mail, because I've almost forgotten what courtesy means. This is a 24/7 news channel, after all: we have other things to worry about. And most of the real stories, keep in mind, don't come from public relations types. Though you never quite know when something's going to land in your lap.

But she smiles, like I've just given her the key to my palace. I'm curious to know why she thought I'd give a shit about chicks with UTI, in the first place.

'I was told you look at women's issues sometimes, ma'am.'

24 BROKEN NEWS

The ma'am used to get to me, but then I realised, I'm getting on in years, there's no point telling the freshers to just use my first name. Call me M, I used to say, and they'd give me an uncomprehending look half the time. 'Okay ma'am, M,' they'd blush and smile.

And well, even if it's not full-on respect, maybe I've earned that ma'am, you know?

Now I give Janki the fake frozen smile, dismissing her. I'm thinking ahead to my next bulletin. There's just about an hour to go; I better start scanning the wires, see the latest info that's being flashed and start working on the show run-down. I call a couple of the reporters to check on their updates . . . you have to put in the effort to get a solid news bulletin. Though, of course, there are days when I've gone in zero motivation, zero preparation. It can get mundane sometimes; but what a rush, when you've done a good show. All tingly nerves and excitement.

And somehow you have to make sure to save enough of you, save enough energy so you don't look like a bundle of nerves on air, so you project enough authority and calm to look credible, never mind what's screwing up behind the scenes as you speak! As good as you get, it always wants more. The great beast is now hungry 24/7 in this country, and that means you better be on your toes, even if you're not sent out to bring in the big breaking news.

Which to be perfectly honest, I'm not. But slap a layer of gloss on that bitterness, and you wouldn't know it to look at me; I'm on air after all, so what am I bitching about, right?! That's what my friends keep reminding me. Got to stay fabulous, don't you know. It's not like I'm one of the yokels doing all the backbreaking labour and never getting a bit of recognition.

And to my credit, I'm finally somewhat immune to the nasty comments. When they say you need a thick skin for this job, they're certainly not kidding. I've trained myself now, have learned to ignore the patronising bullcrap, the whole dismissive, 'Oh M, yes she's a *lovely* girl', with the unsaid, 'Let's leave it at that, never mind the IQ'. All I register these days, is I'm on air, whoever's bitching me out is not, and that's all there is to it. It's pretty ironic, actually, considering I was always the smart one, in school and college. It's only when I'd just joined here, they would try and tell me I'm attractive, just not too smart. I guess it's because no one can quite figure out why *you're* on TV, and they're not.

And don't get me started on co-anchors. From getting jittery that you've got too much air-time, to stealing your lines on air, to going green over how many promos you have compared to him/her—it can all take a toll!

Not to mention eat away at your self-confidence.

'You look terrible in that colour'. 'Why does your jaw stick out that way?' 'Why do you talk so fast?' 'Why are you so slow?' 'You looked so lost on air today. Do you even know what you're talking about?' 'You've been here three years and have no fucking sense of TV, get out of my sight!' And 'Did you see her hair? On air! What was she thinking!' All this within plain sight of whoever is around.

There's no way this criticism isn't personal. The girls getting bitchy—it's unfortunate, but that we're all socially conditioned to handle that. But bitchy men? Bitchy, pot-bellied, balding, insecure men who would as soon knife your ambitions as smile at you. I'll tell you what, the trick is to smile right back. It's all about the airtime, baby.

I'm dismissive now, but it used to make me physically

nauseous. There was so much to get used to. I had to groom myself, worry about style *and* keep track of that little thing that makes us all tick: the news. It's insane. Insane pressure.

I don't think I can tell Janki this, though I do want to warn her . . . but how do you shit on someone's dreams like that?

Someone told me and I must remember to repeat this to Janki: 'You can't trust anyone's opinion here. Just assume if you're not hearing people bitch about the work you're doing, you're doing well. If you screw up, you'll definitely hear about it!'

But it goes the other way too, if people are ripping you apart, you might be doing a little too well. That's another golden rule—wait, is anyone writing these down!

You put up with it all cause you're on top, in a sense. And the beauty of this job is the medium—you reach people, you get to make a difference, at least sometimes, with stories or series. But from this perch, I can tell you, you also run the risk of a complete disconnect with normal life . . . And sometimes, the fear of falling to the bottom of the heap punches you in the gut. I don't even want to look down, it makes me dizzy. Nowadays I hide the fact that I'm sneakily looking over my shoulder, hoping I don't fuck up.

I swivel back around and stare into my screen, oblivious to the chatter of the news room—it's just so much background noise, you only really pick up on stuff happening when the decibel levels rise, and when it's breaking news, well that's when there's a crackling amount of energy—people running around, getting things done, people yelling to get those things done, people focused—

none of this comes on air, of course, just the big bold letters 'breaking news'.

My chat buddy Neville pings me. He works round the corner, at another TV channel. There's no ego clash, no rivalry though ... he's not in front of the camera, and I don't find him snotty in the least. He's pleasant-looking too, so I'm not ruling anything out, not just yet.

N: 'sup, babe?

M: not frikkin much—sooo bored out of my frikkin skull can't even tell u

N: want to sneak out for a quick drink?

M: i wish, have a bulletin in 20

N: well let me know after, I'm here yawning my way thru the day

M: lol, will do.

I close the chat window as surreptitiously as possible when I see our paunchy boss Samit walk by the desks facing mine. He hasn't seen me yet, and it's not like it's illegal to chat in office, and not like I'm giving anything away—which they'd soon enough know, seeing as they monitor all our emails and internet activity! But wherever you are in the world, it doesn't look good when you're sitting, dicking around on the net ... unless you look industrious. It's all about the image: if you look like you're flaking, you're a flake. If you constantly look busy, headless-chicken style like my colleague Chandrika has perfected the art of, well, the boss thinks you're an industrious little beaver. It's that simple.

Never mind that she's a conniving mega-bitch and, in fact, does squat.

I get my focus back, tighten up my anchor links, get ready for a final touch-up before going up to the studio. And we're on air ... in thirty seconds, ten ... cue.

3. *It Gets Personal*

Well, as things turned out, I didn't have time to savour my new-found mentor status for long. The very next day was a miserable one. News of the Big Break-Up had filtered through the office. Months later, but that didn't make it any easier to deal with.

Seems to me, a particular kind of bottom-feeder thrives in the TV news environment. It's not a very lofty calling, I know, but here *more* so than anywhere else that I can think of. On the outside, you're given to believe that the media is the most empowered part of society, the most out-there, the most liberal—the people who Give a Shit, in short, about issues, human rights, about tragedy . . .

It's bullshit.

For instance a senior editor's take on the issue of saffron terror, 'Serves everyone right these Hindu fundos are giving a call to arms—we've spent way too long appeasing those Mozzies'. (I heard that, going into a news bulletin . . . thank god for our reporters on the ground, just sticking to dishing out the information bias-free.)

Or the trial by media in the investigation into the murder of a fourteen-year-old. The father, the monster, the headlines screamed. The mother and father bad parents, one channel proclaims. No one quite knew what had happened, but never mind the facts: the media's at hand to lynch people. In newsrooms across the country, experienced journalists furiously debated the mother's possible guilt. 'Did you see her giving the interviews?'

'Not natural, I mean, no signs of sadness. Her daughter was just killed.'

'So creepy, yaar. Imagine parents like that.'

The point is, if people aren't going to have their hearts in the right place when it comes to the big human rights' issues, there's no hope on the basic *human* issues, is there?

And how sad that it's only when it's personal that I even bother to stop and register this.

It's hard to keep yourself clean and gossip-free, at the best of times. People are constantly trying to size you up, fit you in their little boxes, but above all, get some dirt on you. Guys with egos the size of giant melons looking to pick you up . . . they assume you're easy because you're in TV after all! If you don't sleep with them, you're a snob and a frigid tight-ass; if you do, you're a slut. Especially if you have the balls to do it openly. Most of the girls I know are, well, forced to hide the fact.

Remain virginal till the end, that's the spirit.

As for me, I wouldn't mind being called a slut as much as a sucker, you know.

I'm digressing, I know. I don't really want to address any of this stuff with Vikram, not really. We'd both been pretty low-key during the break-up in August, so I suppose it's a good thing people are only beginning to hear the sordid story now. But it is humiliating, even if it was about six months ago.

PRE-BREAKDOWN 33

Cringe. You know what I mean, if you've ever been cheated on. I'm not your doe-eyed, wilting flower type, by any stretch of the imagination, and even so, to be made a complete ass out of!

Well, fine, I'll just get this off my chest, seeing as my best office friend Deepa's already heading towards me, eyes all big and limpid with concern.

Ugh.

She takes me out for a smoke.

'Are you okay?' she asks.

She never asks me that, it's part of our unwritten code. We're the kick-ass Amazons; we never get rattled.

'Sure,' I go for blasé.

'Well, people are talking about Vikram again. He just came to office for, like, a half-hour this morning with that bitch.'

Technically, his new squeeze is not the bitch in the situation, I suppose, but of course she is to me and mine.

'That's okay, man, it's been over for so bloody long, Deeps,' I say, in a tone that makes a mockery of the bravado I'm going for.

'Umm, yeah, also ... well, it's not just that you know ... it's the Facebook stuff, as well, I guess,' she trails off into a focused examination of her cigarette, as I try not to sputter.

WTF? I charge back in to check my computer.

So it's been months and months, and Vikram and I were both incredibly discreet at first about the split. I never told him how hurt I was by the whole thing (except for three whiny emails right at the outset), but my pride grew into a cast-iron shell. Credit to me, I suppose, that no one picked up on the betrayal or my life falling apart, even though I walked around looking like death. Okay, they might have picked up on me looking like death—this is TV after all—but couldn't really figure out why. Hell, my friends only got to know when I updated my Google chat status to 'Game Over'. Literally.

And now, *this*. What a fucking nightmare. It seems the putz has gone and updated all his info on Facebook. In graphic detail. And with some explicit photos up there, of his butt plug of a new squeeze and him.

I suppose word of his cheating (on me) would have stayed under wraps if his now-cheat-ee Suparna (he apparently two-timed her as well) hadn't been posting crap on his wall.

Serves him right.

But then I check and she's writing stuff on mine too, as of today. WTF?

Here's one I delete—and god knows who's seen that before I erase it forever:

When he told you he loved me how dare you go on to fuck him in our bedroom, you whore

I have no idea what she's talking about. Unless . . . was that West End house we were renting *hers*? God, I think I just threw up a little bit, back into my own throat.

He was always a bit of a skank, I suppose, but you never see the spots when you're looking the damn leopard in the face, you know? They tell you they're changing and blink a couple of times, and fools like me believe it.

Back in the day, we were pretty happy. Plain and simple. We went everywhere together: clubbing, eating out, friends' places, cosy little trips to Manali, Ladakh,

Mumbai, the Andamans, you name it. And after two-and-a-half years, he proposed to me beautifully. And I'm not even the cheesy type who believes in happily ever after!

We'd planned this trip last May to Paris, because it had been my dream for so long. You know that whole Eiffel Tower fixation, the Arc de Triomphe, the whole *Casablanca* reference.

'So let's go,' he'd said. 'I can't believe you've never been. You belong on the Champs-Elysées.'

He had a way with words, the bastard.

That thing they tell you about listening to your gut, well a word to the wise, it's hard-wired into us, a survival instinct . . . ignore at your peril. But I ignored it all, that gnawing fear, the hints from common friends about Suparna—who *he* said was his slightly demanding friend, but a 'very sweet chick, M, you'll love her'. They told me she had a massive crush on him and, well, they didn't want to say, but Vikram and she did spend a lot of time together, no?

The gradual distance between us, I put down to our manic schedules . . . I didn't want to see it, I guess.

In any case, now, we'll never have Paris. Prophetic gut or no, France never happened. At the last minute, Vikram had to go to a conference in New York the exact week we were planning to get away.

J'etais désolée.

But what does he do but book me on a flight with him, and bang in the middle of his work trip, in the middle of Times fuckin' Square, the mecca of all that consumerist glory, when I had my eyes peeled for the naked cowboy (whom I never got to see), well, he popped the question.

It was perfect.

At least, what I heard of it was perfect. Something like, 'Do you want to just do this thing?'

I thought it was very well put.

I was in love.

Those were great times. We came home happy, on an all-time high, personally. Work-wise, Vikram got straight into his special series on the Indo–US nuclear deal in June. And the timing, of course, was perfect—the government staked its political life on the deal, and the confidence motion happened in July.

It was all very dramatic, and we were in the middle of all the news. The industry, I'm telling you, was literally abuzz. That's enough to give you a kick right there—sure, we're never supposed to *be* the story, when we're reporting or anchoring, but there's something about delivering that news, whether it's in print or on TV, to be honest, that's a whole lifetime away from reading it in the papers the next morning. You feel a part of the whole process, and that's a kick, ninety-nine per cent of the time.

And when your better half's breaking news on this sort of stuff, it's a high of its own. The Left, disgruntled, but out in the cold, had not much to say— for a while at least. Vikram's main rival at work was the soon-to-be-insignificant Left reporter, so that meant more glory and airtime for Vik; he was the happiest person around. And by extension, so was I. He sounded all charged up whenever we spoke. I was told that was mirrored across most every channel, and later, when the deal was officially pushed through, reporters and anchors acted as if they'd overcome some personal milestone—only by then my world had bottomed out.

I was doing bulletins every day the month it happened. Focusing on speaking clearly, getting the full three-sixty on everything that was going on. Three lives with three reporters in just the first segment of one bulletin ... the Valley burning ... and the politicians twisting the knives, exacerbating the differences, hoping to lure in the votes. Fundo groups holding protests across the major cities of north India. Meanwhile the president of Pakistan—soon to be former president of Pakistan, did he know it yet?— was making incendiary comments, trying to take advantage of Jammu and Kashmir burning, ignoring the threat of impeachment hanging over his head. A massive voter turnout would ensure that the people had the final say, but that was still a couple of months away.

This then, was the news the day my little world fell apart. Vikram and I had all but moved in together into this gorgeous house in West End: well beyond *my* budget, but what's a nearly-married girl to do, right? We'd checked it out, pretty much signed off on it, and I was elated—just moving from east Delhi to the heart of south Delhi, with the man I loved, would do it, but on top of that, it felt like things were coming together beautifully.

And then, after a particularly long day, I walked in to find—nothing flashy like another chick's panties or anything; something much more banal—a gift not meant for me, and the remains of a meal for two in the sink. Wait, I think it was sticking out of the trash.

Whatever.

I knew in a second.

It took me more than a couple to get out though. I'd been so close. So close to the perfect ending.

Looking back, it could have been *anyone*; a dinner with a colleague perhaps, an old friend. But what can I tell you, what's left of your heart plunges into your intestines and from a new, lower centre of gravity, you know for sure.

I didn't even wait for him to get back before I started packing.

'What the hell are you doing,' his eyes widening, as I barged past him into the hallway, big black Samsonite gripped tight.

'Don't give me that,' I snapped. Too dazed to know what was going on, what I was walking out on. 'I've heard enough of your excuses . . . Tell me Suparna wasn't here.'

And as he answered, smooth as can be, I knew right then, the truth about Vikram, whom I'd believed all along, because why would he want to marry me otherwise? If he didn't love me?

I don't even remember what he had to say, the gift was for me? He'd opened it and meant to re-seal it? It didn't matter. The first thing I did, after walking out of that West End house, was drag a close-enough friend at the time to a discreet little clinic in Haus Khas, to get checked. For all the usual claptrap, HIV, Hep A and C and gonorrhoea. Sexually transmitted rage isn't something you can screen for, alas.

It's a scene straight out of *Reality Bites*, it is, but there's no frikkin' Ethan Hawke on the horizon, not that I can see. Luckily, my friend's done this before so she holds my hand and keeps her wits about her. Just from the way the word sounds, I'm convinced I have gonorrhoea. Luckily not, as I find out a day later.

But hurtling me right back into the present, someone's

calling my name, everything's blurring around me. I'm not even crying, I don't think. Omg. *This* is just too much. Hysterical blindness. Deepa's saying something to me. I look at her, and have absolutely no clue what she's babbling on about. I walk out of the room that's too dazzlingly bright for my eyes, for my nerves, into the foyer.

Till now, I've been one of those slightly smarmy, superior types no one's really had too much on. I commiserate in chorus, when we hear about the girls who've been burned by their asshole-boyfriends. And I can just predict how my guy friends are going to react, their hitherto-buried chivalry coming to the fore: 'I would never have treated you like that. D'you want me to pound him?'

The girls are more like, 'Oh no, poor you, the bastard, how could we not have known? Don't worry she's a slut, he'll get what's coming to him.' But mixed in with that pity, is our own paranoia, that this is exactly what will happen to us too.

I've been in *that* group, on the outside, never on this side, the one people are gossiping about. There was just that one little cloud: five years ago, I slept with one of the senior execs—something I never confirmed or denied—but that's long done and forgotten. I avoid the married dudes now, and stay out of harm's way.

Now this. I knew this would come back and bite me in the ass. This entire Vikram episode—it was all too public. We're both in the public sphere now, whether we like it or not. Never, never shit where you eat, I want to tell my younger self. Stay away from the incestuous media family where everyone's doing everyone else.

Ugh.

Of course, Vikram's doing better than fine now. And the fact that he's a prime-time anchor sleeping with the boss of one of the newly-launched entertainment channels, no less—it's just the proverbial icing on the cake. He's nothing if not a mover. I used to love that about him—mistaking the convenience for coincidence—his knack of getting the timing right in just about everything, his innate ability to charm all my friends. It's just the way he's built. He knows how to get along with the people he needs to get along with, does my ex.

But finally, finally, I've gotten over the gloom and desperation and the inward silent screaming, and the nausea and the not eating, and *now* is when people realise?

How will I ever get any work done today? And I'm supposed to be working on a half-hour show on slum children, which I've been dawdling on.

I suppose it's crisis intervention that Deepa's here for. She's got me by the collar practically, dragging me off to the bathroom because I'm sniffling into my sleeve. Crying. In public. A big no-no, where we come from. Yes, that's right, the stereotype of the weak, crying, emotional woman doesn't quite fly in this space.

'Hey, what's going on? Babe, everyone's talking about you, pull yourself together!' she says, pretty damn sternly, if you ask me, for someone who's been pouring her heart and soul out about *her* break-up every couple of days for the past two months.

'I *have* it together, just that everyone is talking about that idiot,' I mumble. 'And about me.'

'That's not something you can control . . .' she starts.

PRE-BREAKDOWN 41

I glare at her in the mirror.

'Give me a second to get over it, for fuck's sake,' I say, getting some authority back into my tone.

'It's just a momentary thing, don't worry,' she says. 'Don't let them see they've got you, remember?' I'd told her exactly that when people were whispering about her marriage being called off at the last second because she's a manglik or some crap.

'Hmm, thanks, I'm okay.' I yank my arm out of her grasp; I really want no emotion here. Deepa's gotten good at giving me my space when I need to clamp up, internalise and deal with shit. Which is why I'm surprised she feels the need for an intervention today. But I tune her out. Splash some water on my face, turn my mind into a solid plate of glass—it's a good trick, you must let me show you some time—and walk out.

Deepa walks me to my desk and says I should come with her for an editorial meeting. We have these meetings every morning and early evening, and I usually sneak out of them. But she's been telling me that, as a mid-level anchor, I need to increase my in-house visibility so people will start taking me more seriously. She thinks I should start pushing to do prime-time shows now. Someone must have fed her that, probably our boss, Samit, the senior features editor. It's so not a line she'd come up with on her own. He'd been hoping to see me take on more responsibility, he'd told me last year, he wanted me to slowly pick up the reins and take charge of a team. The ensuing fall-out of the relationship wasn't conducive to what he had in mind—I barely had the mind-space to deal with my own job profile, let alone take on any more.

I used to clock fourteen hours a day, no joke, three to four times a week. My heart was in this thing, you know. To the exclusion of all else. But when I had to cope with my life falling apart, though I still put in my time, I let go a little. I guess Samit feels I let him down.

I'm sure my attitude doesn't help. Even with meetings— I mean, they're definitely not high on my list of priorities: either they can see my work and judge me on that, or they can take a hike. Deepa joined a little later than me, though, and she's still a little edgy about what's proper and what's not. Well, after all, it was a protocol issue that made her leave her last job. The boss kept hitting on her and when she rebuffed him, he threw the book at her in many ways, or rather, got his underlings to do it. She's extra-careful to stay squeaky clean here, and following the rules is definitely more her personality type.

'Fine, fine, I'm there in, like, two seconds,' I growl at her. 'You carry on, I'll be there in a bit.' Yeah right, on a day like today. My ass. I have more important things to do, like—a little belatedly—put all my office friends on a limited profile list. And erase whatever personal stuff is on Facebook. And then I'll slink out of office ostensibly for a recce for my *Slumdog Millionaire*-related story. Now that the movie is making such waves world-wide, every second special show has some *Slumdog* angle.

I'll come back to work, I figure, when the storm's blown over; fortunately, I know that everyone might be gossiping their asses off right now, but the attention span's not too long. As long as I stay under the radar! Soon enough, there'll be something else to talk about, for instance, who was caught making out with whom at the office party (the

PRE-BREAKDOWN 43

big-shot visiting bureau chief with the young intern, and two guys from the foreign desk with each other, shirts off and all).

It's just so much easier to be charitable when you're not in the middle of it. It's all tangled up, my pride and my hurt and my aching heart—even though technically I've been seeing someone else for the past month or so. But Neeraj, the young gorgeous metro reporter, is not one for emotional depth, at least I don't see him that way. Not much of a support system that way. Not a patch on Vikram.

But now, snap back, I'm reading my two news bulletins for the day, it's all slumdogs and pre-election fever, politics and entertainment, with some sports in between. The most uninspiring shows I've ever done, reading straight from the tele-prompter, not changing a single word, not asking a single intelligent question, not bothering in the least about the news.

I shouldn't be here.

I leave office for Ankita's house and sofa in Green Park: a place that is inviting, non-judgemental, and most importantly, not hooked up to the Net, so I can't obsessively track the twists and turns of my peer-sponsored desolation online.

4. Hairline Cracks and the Rhythm

Ankita gets home only by about eight or nine at night—I'm splayed out on the couch. Not a pretty sight. 'Hey,' she says, 'did you eat something?'

Ever the host. I mumble something about not being hungry. 'Just remind me that no one cares, Ankita, it's been months now,' I say, trying to command something, some poise, some self-assurance.

'Of course it doesn't matter now. You've crossed that bump on the road, this is just a cloud of crap—you'll breeze on through, baby,' she reassures me.

But I don't think I will, I don't think I can, and I can't let on, that having Vikram in the picture has blow-torched my heart again, never mind what anyone says.

Ankita's making us a stiff drink each, but I'm not in the mood for conversation or commiseration, I can't be here, I feel claustrophobic. We call me a cab, and I head home.

I've already cut three calls from Neeraj this evening. I just send him a message saying, *'hey, i'll call in a bit, x'*. I can't deal right now, simply not possible. He's been great fun, but just not long-term mould; you don't always need 'fun' when everyone else your age is going for serious and settled.

48 BROKEN NEWS

I get home, and the memories are a battering ram. I thought I'd left the grief behind me ages ago—it's vestigial grief, I'm sure, almost-nostalgic memories of heartache. No doubt aided by the fact that, for the last month—since my former roommate Nisha has gone to get help for alcohol addiction—I've been coming home day after day to a cold, empty house and dragging myself out of bed, it seems, just minutes after collapsing into it.

This whole urban, empowered life is really a one-way track to suicide city, sometimes, is what I think.

But what do I know, I'm just grey and old and jaded.

The only things that made sense in the aftermath of the break-up were the songs I eventually couldn't get off my iPod fast enough. Moby's *Dream about Me*. Some Beyoncé, but she has more going on than I ever will. One Republic wailing, *'It's too late to apologise'*, and of course I'm sitting there thinking oh god I wish he would . . . I wish he'd realise and come back, and we'd start over.

The first few months after the break-up were a whirl of endless appointments and eighteen-hour workdays, of flashing dazzling smiles all the time, but watching the cracks on the inside grow and spread and take on a life of their own. I forced myself to go out at night, and there was something manic in the way I smiled and socialised— there was a desperation that poured out of me.

I got enough action: don't get me wrong. There was something chemical oozing out of me, and all of a sudden they were all over it, the guys—just the wrong kind of guys.

I took three weeks off in November, ostensibly to travel, but really to have a little bit of a meltdown away from prying eyes. My two best friends, Ankita and Karthik, kept me in booze and pot for long enough for me to finally get a grip on reality, go figure.

The terror attacks put shit in perspective. I was in Mumbai at the time, sucked into this surreal vortex with the rest of the country for sixty hours, watching bleary-eyed and soul-shaken as terrorists held Mumbai hostage. Many friends of friends were counting their blessings that day—a narrow escape. Nothing like death and destruction to put your crummy life problems in perspective.

I tried to pour my heart and soul into work, when I got back, over Christmas and New Year's, but somehow nothing really seemed to click. Sure I was doing fairly well, but nothing stellar. I guess I cheered up somewhat only in early January, when the rebound happened with Neeraj. He was incredibly sweet, so I let him take me out, and the rest of it.

We weren't exclusive at first, more off and on ... At least, there was a movie slash dinner date, and maybe, most crucially, another warm body in bed. He was good too, which always helps. And I have to say, from what I know of most Indian men, courtesy surveys and several, well, experiments over the years, they're not too big on the foreplay, so it's nice this younger breed is part alpha male, part metro-sexual and fully attuned to your needs. He's a good kid. And had no issues keeping it subtle and far from prying eyes—we haven't made the gossip lists, which is nice.

I know Neeraj is a good guy, and he's with me, but it's not the real deal. I see what the realisation is, that I was racing away from, in my desperation to avoid the heartbreak and solitude. It's taken *this*, a mauling of my carefully-constructed defences, to make me realise it's *me* who failed somehow. Let's face it, my last real relationship ended badly six months ago, and I'm not done mourning it.

And what a riot—I'm the person dishing out relationship advice to my girlfriends. To Ankita, who's been sucked into a vortex of matrimonial ads and clandestine meetings, with her parents actively edging her out of their little nest.

Just last weekend, at a family lunch with Ankita and her mum, our parents tch-tching away over how this generation has no staying power.

'There's something a little wrong with her,' Ankita's mother Leena tells my mum, in a hushed tone, when Ankita's in the kitchen. 'She's becoming insecure and bitter.'

'These girls, what are they thinking, waiting for so long.' My mum at her helpful best. 'But then again, Leena, at least they have their jobs, their careers. Options we never had,' she goes on.

I'm no help to Ankita any more—I used to encourage her to fight it out, to meet the dorks through these marriage portals but to keep her sanity intact, and know the choice is ultimately hers. But it takes a toll, that I've seen.

She used to think me and Vikram were the great hope, that maybe she too would meet 'the one'. But my way's no better than hers. Hook up, break up, hook up, break up. With no one around to help you pick up the pieces.

Either way, you're screwed.

But this morning, waking up, I decide I have to fight it

out. 'I can handle it. I can handle it', that's the mantra I'm chanting to myself, keeping my most charming, fakest smile on my face. But then, as I walk in to office, I start to register the sympathy on people's faces.

Barf-o-rama.

Janki accosts me in the hallway now, with something about something, god knows what. 'Will you look at it, then? I don't have that much time to figure out with . . .' she's saying.

'Yeah, yeah, okay.' I'm edging away from her, trying to hold on to an iota of professional pride here, no clue what's going on.

I suppose people are now done gossiping and are at that feeling bad for me stage. Whatever it is, I'm still on their radar, which makes me super-uncomfortable. I just want to blend back into nothingness. A wall-flower introvert stuck in this mad extravagant spectacle of TV—something's gotta give.

I don't have too much time for neurosis, it's the day *Slumdog Millionaire* sweeps the Oscars. Phenomenal, *eight* Oscars. I have a couple of news shows to anchor, and it's all very heady.

In our meetings, we're figuring out what shows we can do around this—the evening prime-time show is to be an entertainment bonanza, reporters and producers trying to make sure we get the teams involved on the phone line, or through a live satellite uplink from Los Angeles, as well as some from Mumbai. The big interviews are happening in LA of course, but we're going to drive what we can, with inputs from families of the big Oscar winners, whether it's A.R. Rahman's sister in Chennai, or Resul Pookutty's wife and children in Kerala.

I'm trying to help with the research and volunteer to help script and cut a couple of the packages for the show. It gets me out of my head, which is always a good thing. But it's not just today. Deepa and I are in charge of planning a series of stories, on this and on the *Smile Pinki* guys, the documentary that also won an Oscar. It's all pretty exciting.

Janki comes up to me again, she wants some attention. 'Is there anything I can help out with?' she asks.

'Hey no, not really, we have this under control,' I start to say, but see that's not the answer she's looking for. 'Why don't you sit in with us as we're editing it though, just to get a sense of how it all comes together.'

She makes a face. Not a good sign. 'Oh, edits I've seen enough of,' she tells me, sourly. I guess because she's being put through the grind of regular desk work. No one finds the editing or shooting process quite as glamorous as the rest.

'It's not the same as editing those news stories, Janki,' I try to tell her, but give up. 'Okay, well if you're not interested in that, you can always come in when we're rolling the show live tonight. Come to the PCR.'

'Uh, ok,' she makes an effort to sound interested. 'So you're not anchoring it or anything?'

'No, no, it's being done out of Mumbai,' I tell her, and want to add that it's not all about fronting a show—the back-end stuff is pretty critical. But I don't have the time or energy right now.

I do palm her off, though, onto Rahul, my anchor boss, no less, who's striding into the room, owning it the moment he walks in, the way he always does.

PRE-BREAKDOWN 53

'Rahul, I wonder if you've met Janki,' I tug at his sleeve.

'Hey M,' he smiles at me. Janki gets a 'Hi', as he waits for me to say something.

'Isn't this incredible, this Oscar fever!' I gush. 'Oh and Janki here is very interested in working on other roles besides the desk,' I add. 'Maybe if you have space in one of your workshops?' Rahul holds in-house workshops from time to time, to find and nurture undiscovered on-air talent. It's pretty cool, actually, and part of his job profile, as senior anchor. He's also someone who takes mentoring seriously—I mean, he wanted to mentor me for years!

'Hey yeah, sure,' he says. 'Why don't you mail me what sort of space you're interested in,' he tells her, and then strides off.

Janki looks stunned, she's still yet to say a word. I pat her on the shoulder and turn back to my work.

Deepa just rolls her eyes. She's not quite as impressed with Janki as I was initially. 'You're taking an interest in her, but there's no point,' she says laconically. 'She just wants to be where you are.' Deepa always has the strangest insights into people.

I reject that outright. 'Hey, I'm just thinking, how cool would it have been to have someone do some hand-holding when I joined, you know,' I explain. And why not be nice to her, if she's a bright young thing.

Except she doesn't show up to the PCR, and Deepa and I forget all about her in our manic drive to get everything right, as the show rolls live.

It's a tiring day, but so worth it. And to top it all off, by evening, I've convinced Samit's boss and the editorial head of the team—I don't see Samit anywhere—to let me do a special panel discussion show out of Mumbai for the weekend. I'm pretty happy about it. Not just because of the show, but also because it'll hide me.

I realise belatedly that I haven't called Neeraj back. I haven't seen him around either, but figure I should at least let him know I'll be flying to Mumbai the next day. I really want to explain that I'm not ignoring him, I just need some space—and to be honest, it's only so long before they start gossiping about me and him as well. It's all very Mrs Robinson—he's in his early twenties, after all. He is doing a stand-up job, no doubt, but he still has a way to go.

And at some level, I'm not sure I'm ready to deal with the stuff he needs to get out of his system: the networking, the partying, trendy places. 'He knows all the coolest clubs in Delhi, and which day you have to be seen at which one,' I'd told Ankita. And I wasn't quite as excited about that as it sounds. I'm an old bird now—my idea of excitement is a late movie on a Friday night.

But yeah, as I told her, I suppose the sex makes up for it all.

Just that you figure when you want such dramatically different things—for him, it's the relationship that's exciting, for me, where it's all going to lead (not to forget that my eggs have been dying the last five to six years)—it's best not to confuse the issue.

He's been trying to get me to talk to him, let him help me through these past few days, but I've just shut down. Shut him out. I can't do it.

I pick up the phone to call him, but wimp out and send him a text instead.

PRE-BREAKDOWN 55

'I'm going out of town for a show for a couple of days. Sorry been so out of it. Let's chat when I'm back.'

'Ok fine.'

That's the reply! I guess he's not too thrilled with me. Not that I blame him. Anyway, I'm on my way home, crashing early and it's Maximum City, baby!

My first stop after I land in Mumbai, is the bagel place off Carter Road, to meet my college-friend-turned-friendly-rival, Preeti. We'd been very close at one point, but sort of grew apart—in fact, we haven't even spoken to each other for a while. We always get a bit competitive, as I'd said, but whatever. I'm here in Mumbai for a show, she's here on holiday—it all clicks. Preeti's not changed a bit; she's actually pretty much as you see her on TV— glamorous, always made-up à la latest mode, and though I secretly used to find that a bit put-on, it's refreshing to see, now, when I feel like everything's shaken around me.

Some constancy.

'He did what!' she says, once we settle down with our mango shakes and massive bagels (plain cream cheese for her, avocado for me). Sitting in the tiny alfresco section, we're constantly facing a barrage of noise, but the food and the breeze make up for it.

'Well, he's a total ass-wipe, he's just gone and broadcast his fucking relationship with that woman to the whole world. Pictures and all.' I can be quite calm, talking about this now, but that underlying rage isn't going anywhere. 'Not to mention that Suparna chick slagging me off online.'

'God, so much for waiting forever.'

'What?'

56 BROKEN NEWS

'Oh.' She looks unabashed. 'I'd sort of . . . meant to tell you then, but Vikram called me last year, around Christmas, and told me to talk to you, you know to forgive him and shit.'

'What? You never told me!' I'm not liking this.

'Well, I'd just met you after you split up, and you were doing so well. Don't you remember—we'd just hit a club after two in the morning or something, you were out after ages, and I didn't want to shake that up.' She sounds like she's trying to convince me, and I can feel the anger rising.

'But Preeti, don't you think you should have at least let me know what he said?!'

'But he was totally insincere, don't you see?' she says, and well, I guess she's known him as long as I have, I can only hope not as intimately, though you never know with that dirt-bag.

'No, I don't see,' I say into my drink and find my hand shaking a little when I light up my tenth cigarette of the morning.

'Well, he said he'd wait forever for you to change your mind,' she ploughs on, 'and it's not even been, what, seven months, and he's obviously moved on, the bastard.'

Slight pause.

He said he'd wait.

'Oh, honey, honey, are you okay?'

Yeah, not my finest hour. I'm crying away now, all stupid pent-up feeling. Why the hell didn't he wait? I would have forgiven him. I know I would have. And then I start feeling pathetic *for* that—what am I, a doormat?

'Why does bad shit happen to good people,' I say

PRE-BREAKDOWN   57

pleadingly, and we both crack up. We've been making fun of books and people saying shit like that since we were much, much younger.

What can I say, I'm on an emotional see-saw here.

I have to head into work, so the momentary hysteria's where we leave it, but I make plans to meet her for a night on the town. We're recording the show the next day, and I know I probably should have come straight into office, but what the hell . . . no one knows me here—I mean they *know* me from on-air stuff, but at least no one senior is checking up on me. I have to leave the office almost immediately though, because the stylist insists I get my measurements taken at this chi-chi designer boutique, which assures me they'll be able to modify a gorgeous outfit for me in time.

This is Mumbai we're talking about, so it's some four hours or some interminable travel time before I'm back in the office where I know no one, but someone smiles and chats with me, so I end up borrowing his computer to log on and check in with work. I also charge my cellphone— I hadn't had a chance to do so befoe I left for the airport, and the thing had died on me.

There are a couple of offline messages from Neville, my chat buddy.

N: where have you got to hotshot?

N: missing you in this corner . . . let me know when you're free, we shd totally get tht drink

Less fun, in my official ID, are forty-five emails. There's a series of mails from Deepa, who starts out fine but gets increasingly frantic.

This morning.

58 BROKEN NEWS

Hi M, hope you had a good flight and you're feeling better. Love and hugs, D.

Two hours later.

M, your phone's still off, so I'm guessing you haven't landed yet. Things here in office are fine, just call me when you can.

Afternoon.

M, what the f! Office has been trying to get hold of you—they wanted something, not sure exactly what. Didn't you tell Samit you were off to Bom??

And then

Dude, boss is pissed off, call immediately!

I call her immediately.

'Hi, what's—' I start, but she cuts in.

'—Listen, for some reason, Samit took off at the meeting about how he's not sure why we had to fly you into Mumbai for the show when you're needed here for post-Oscar shows and stories. And then that little Janki or whatever, was all like, well sir, I have been training with M ma'am, I can help out.'

'That's crap,' I tell her.

'I know, that's what I told him, because he blew his top, said what the fuck are you doing training people and getting them to, well, cover for you, he said, when you're not getting any other work done for your team.'

'Is he mad? I'm going to call him this second. He knows for a fact that I was told to come to Mumbai and record this show, for the weekend,' I tell her. 'What's really going on?'

'I'm not sure, but it's weird. And all of a sudden that Janki is strutting around. What's the deal with that?'

'That's okay, she's not important, Deeps, I'll just talk to

Samit. I'll figure it out,' I tell her, quite perturbed that my little working holiday has been shaken up already. 'Talk soon.'

I text Samit as soon as I get off the phone with Deepa: *Hi, in Mumbai office. Working on show, should have rundown in place by later this evening. Is that okay?*

Five minutes later: *Okay.*

I message back, saying thanks and I hope things are fine back at work. I don't know how to bring in the Janki morning fiasco without making it sound like Deepa had told on her.

No reply.

Wank job.

To be honest, Samit was probably pissed off because I went over his head to come here. It wasn't the smartest thing on my part, to forget to let him know. But what the hell, it's not like I'm not working.

I set to work on the show in earnest. It involves a lot of groundwork from the team here. We're talking to some of the people in Dharavi, some in Bandra—school kids, teachers, actors, and a couple of people from the movie *Slumdog Millionaire* itself.

I'm quite excited to be working on the show. The features team here will handle the outdoor shoots, which I'll help oversee editorially. I'm going to be doing the in-studio interviews. And we'll spend a couple of days in post-production mode. That doesn't seem like too much, but an anchor has to do some detailed preparation to pull it off. If you're not as prepped as you should be, it's glaringly obvious. I spend the next three hours doing my online research, making calls and emailing a couple of

60 BROKEN NEWS

people from the film industry, as well as talking to our entertainment reporters, who've been all over these stories the second *Slumdog* raised its head.

It's all part of the build-up till the big moment, and if it goes well, it's seamless, or at least appears to be. Only the production team and the editors know how much they slave away to give that illusion. It's a fantastic feeling though—from putting all the blocks together in your head, making the jigsaw fit together mentally, and then . . . watching it all change completely on the edit table. When you do it right, as you watch it come together, especially when you watch it on air, there's nothing like knowing you got it down pat. You have a thread going through the whole show—it has soul.

Or that's the aim, at any rate.

By now it's eight, and I'm quite ready to call it a night. I have my printouts, and I'm heading out of office, even though the guys here seem keen to work till midnight.

Just then, I get a text from Deepa.

Meant to tell you earlier. Janki told us you'd told her how stressed out you are abt whole off gossip thing. Hope you're okay.

WTF! I text back: *What crap! Haven't spoken to her at all.*

She calls me.

'Oh, well, I just thought you might have, you know, since you haven't been talking to me much or Neeraj but—'

I interrupt. 'Are you crazy! Why would I talk to that chick instead of you? And what the hell did Neeraj say to you anyway?' I know Deepa has a soft spot for him, and it's annoying. I get the feeling that she thinks I'm the asshole in this relationship. (She might be on to something there, but I block that thought immediately.)

PRE-BREAKDOWN 61

'Nothing, nothing.' She's very unconvincing. 'He's just concerned about you, M.'

'Wait a minute.' I'm not even worried about Neeraj right now, as the other stuff sinks in. 'She said this in front of Samit or just to you?'

'Well, she said—when she came into our meeting, that is, and he was getting all upset about you being in Mumbai—she said that you're going through a lot.' Deepa's voice sounds a little odd, so I take it the boss didn't react too kindly.

'It's okay, just tell me what he said.'

'He said that everyone goes through shit and he doesn't know why it has to come into the workplace.'

'Oh. Well . . .' I pause. What do you say to that.

'Then Janki said, "No sir, she was talking to me earlier and I feel very bad and all, she was training me, sir, so I'm sure I can help out".'

'Slimy shit.' I'm repelled but strangely fascinated by Janki, now. 'So now the boss thinks I've been whining away instead of working.'

'Hey listen, don't worry, we'll talk to him; I'll talk to him if you like,' she offers.

'Really? I don't know if it'll help. I mean he knows we're close and all, so of course you'll be biased,' I tell her. In fact, Samit had used that closeness once, taking her aside a month or two after we'd become friends, to essentially get her to convey to *me* that I was becoming a bit of a loose cannon, with the 'dodgy company' I was keeping. He'd also said there was no point talking to me himself, *even though he cared*, because I was just stubborn and I had a strange, misplaced sense of loyalty. Basically, he wanted

62 BROKEN NEWS

her to get me to re-think my whole alliance with an ex-colleague and friend Rashmi, who got into a whole lot of shit at work.

'Don't be ridiculous, this girl is lying, she's lying, is all,' Deepa says with some finality.

'Okay. Deeps, I'm going to call it a night. I'll talk to you tomorrow.'

'Okay, good night, don't worry, it'll be fine . . . and have a great show!' I hear her say, as I hang up.

I call Preeti and head for Blue Frog, which I've been told is the most happening place in town, with the best live music—something I definitely don't get enough of in Delhi. There's this band from the UK playing tonight at first, and I love the informality but space of the little pods, and the space out front for the real hard-core dancing. I'm sitting in a pod with Preeti. Her new boyfriend shows up with some friends, and through the evening we get to talking a bit, reminiscing a lot, and then I head to meet a couple of my friends at Hard Rock Café, where there's a boisterous party that we crash. I'm happy to be drinking, not thinking, not bothering with who said what and why and who manipulated whom into which corner . . . in fact, next thing I know, I'm being bundled into an auto and deposited at my hotel at two in the morning, quite the worse for wear. Delhi has no equivalent, as far as I'm concerned.

I barely wake up when the phone beeps loudly the next morning.

It's a text from Deepa: *Morning sweetie, chk ur mail.*

They're already at work, those driven freaks! I would be too, but I have a massive hangover and complete bloating of the gut, thanks to what I'm convinced is food poisoning from an ill-advised omelette at work the previous evening.

And that's not all. When I finally lurch into office, into the make-up room with two hours to go till my show, I find all I have to wear is a very fancy designer magenta kurta-shirt—with a neckline that goes down to my stomach.

Unbelievable.

When I tell you black is my colour, darlings, you'll understand why I had to shut myself in the soundproof booth and scream.

I feel better after that. I pretend that it was my idea to dress up like a tinsel-town diva, and figure I'll handle all the crap they throw at me.

Just two relevant emails, one from Samit saying the rundown should work fine, with two anchor links changed, and one from Deepa, cc Samit, saying she's assigned someone to my show, to get all the B-roll footage done and get graphics and a show sting made back in Delhi.

It's all cool. I go and pep myself up for the show, trying not to feel like I'm out of my element here in Mumbai, with a couple of big names on the show (alas, no super-famous celebrities though). I'm hoping star power doesn't derail me. I don't think it will, judging by the time I spoke to the dashing young politician I've had a crush on forever. The only thing I'm still kicking myself for is not having the savoir faire to go up and chat with him when I saw him at a late night screening of *The Devil Wears Prada*—at a Noida theatre of all places.

But that something extra, the edge, seems to come from the gun mike in your hand and the camera-person in tow. It transforms even the shyest person. Take that away, and

64 BROKEN NEWS

the shoulder pads and blazer, and I'm just the same grungy kid I used to be—just older, is all.

It's not a bad thing. It also helps you keep your sense of self straight. When I'm out with my friends, it's just me. But if I'm going out directly after a shoot, or coming in from a show, there's a sheen of, well, something else: not just because I'm with my team sometimes, but also because we project this air of self-containment, and at times, plain old glamour. We can be glitzy, I'll admit, and authoritative too. It can get intimidating. It can also go to your head and leave you a little delusional, if you ask me, but I crossed that bridge years ago.

It was after I'd been anchoring a while, and I had started getting recognised when we'd go out: clubs and restaurants, and such. It was only when my friend Karthik pulled me aside one day and gave me hell, that I realised I'd been hamming, as if there were adoring fans everywhere. Talking loudly, glancing at myself a whole lot in the mirror, looking to see if there was anyone around who recognised me, not paying enough attention to my friends.

'Preening,' he'd said. 'We're not here on a miserably cold winter day to see you fuckin' preen away.'

'I'm not fucking preening, you asshole,' I'd said, quite offended.

'No, you know what, it's fine. Stop. Stop pretending to be a journalist. Just go ahead, if you want to be the bloody star all the time, go ahead. Just count me and Ankita out,' he spoke on her behalf, but when I looked up at her, she looked pained but in complete agreement.

It killed me.

'Fine, you know what, you can count your bloody selves

out. Anyway, I think you guys are getting damn self-obsessed and bloody judgemental.' I picked up my bag and stomped off. Fuming the entire one hour from Saket in the heart of south Delhi to Mayur Vihar.

They didn't talk to me for two months. Karthik only called me when Ankita's drama at home hit another level, and he thought I should call her. He was completely gruff on the phone, hanging up as soon as he'd told me what was happening. I called him back later that night, after speaking to her on the latest round of emotional blackmail from her parents and extended family.

It was the closest I came to apologising, though I never said anything outright. I felt worse when I found out—through Ankita—that Karthik had wanted to tell us something that night, but I'd been too distracted to realise it. He'd quit his job at the newspaper where he'd worked for some five years, to be a writer. He felt he was running out of time, that he was selling himself short. His parents had thrown a fit, which certainly didn't help, though they were all the way in Kerala. But Karthik went for it anyway . . . and flew out of our lives for a bit, to the back-waters.

My producer's assistant shocks me back into show mode by spilling water all over our leading man—a guy who played a bit role in *Slumdog*. He's having a hissy fit in front of the entire audience, so I just walk in, leverage some authority and get him to calm the fuck down.

I motion that I'm ready to start. The make-up guys come in for the final touch-ups, a little powder so we're not super-shiny on screen. I've already spent half an hour in hair and make-up. Rollers on the top of my head, to get the hair looking big, and they blow-dry it just so. And then iron the ends straight, too. There's some vile foundation to even out the skin, a different shade to make my nose look straight, give my jaw contours and higher cheekbones than god saw fit to give me. Then there's the rouge, the lip outlining—luckily this girl's not like the one in Delhi, who's always looking to give me a super-sultry pout, no matter the hour of day—and lip filling. And then the eyeliner, eye shadow, kajal, eyebrow brushing and my personal favourite—and as far as I'm concerned only necessity—under-eye concealer.

Perhaps this is why it's hard to take it seriously when people compliment you on how you look on TV. In fact, I'm always a little surprised they even recognise me in the first place. There are a handful of women in TV news today who are drop-dead gorgeous, a tiny minority of them who have the brains to boot, with a grasp of the fundamentals of nearly every subject. Those are the real role models as far as I'm concerned. I don't think they give much of a shit about their hair or make-up or clothes. It's all perfunctory, effortless fashion on their part: the really good-looking ones know they could wear a potato sack with big fat orange polka dots and still look fabulous.

Anyway, that's who I pretend I am in my head, super-intelligent-diva me, who takes over and takes complete charge.

It goes pretty well, the show is solid. There's an audience to consider, make eye contact with and project as much authority as I can muster: that's the trick I've figured out; with audience shows, they need to know you're in charge, and then they respond to you. Of course you have to make sure not to let the panellists bully you, or talk over you, and gently but firmly direct the flow of conversation. All this, while keeping track of the voice in your ear counting you down, telling you if you're overtime, and which of the five cameras—apart from the one that is on you constantly—you need to look at.

I'm pleased with my panel, actually, and get caught up in what they're saying. Though, at one point, it's really the done-to-death defensive attitude about having some gora guy come in and shoot our slums—I've gotten sick of the phrase 'poverty porn', and I'm glad some of my guests are equally vocally against it.

I get some great audience input as well, and I know once we edit, it'll be dynamic and pacy. We've shot real-time, so editing shouldn't be too much of a bitch, as it can be when you shoot hours more than you need.

Before you know it, we're done (remember a half-hour show is just some eighteen minutes, minus ads!). I get some charming reactions from my guests after the show, and the college kids in the audience are great too. Two guys ask me out for coffee and a drink, respectively, so I'm not feeling half-bad. Now I have to collect the tapes and get a good editor back in Delhi, and I'm home free. I'm supposed to get a full-fledged producer for this, anyway.

And yet, even as I take my make-up off, I can predict who'll BS me back in the Delhi office: about not giving it that extra edge, talking too fast, talking too slow in bits, not talking enough, not being a carbon copy of so-and-so from the other channel, not being myself enough, not . . . just not measuring up. It can get to you, you know, like the movie stars say, when they're called fat or heavy or histrionic—because it's so damn personal. They're telling

68 BROKEN NEWS

you you're looking fat or not talking right, or picking on you for the way you look, for your hair and size of your nose and god knows what else. I've had it happen before, but it can still take the joy out of my best TV moments.

Luckily, none of the neurosis shows on the outside. It certainly doesn't register on the show reel I've just had made: the broadcast version of a resumé, with our best clips and such. Not that I want to leave my channel— we've grown together in so many ways—but with the industry the way it is, it can't hurt to have an eye out for potential jobs. I'd probably get to ramp up my salary and designation if I wanted.

I check my mail, and am flabbergasted.

Samit has mailed me and Deepa and his boss, the senior editor who allowed me to make the trip, and cc'd the channel head, no less, asking why I was sent to Mumbai at a time when cost-cutting is the operative phrase.

That's ridiculous and unheard of, considering I'm on his team. Sounds like he's making this a discipline issue—just because I didn't tell him? Which I really should have; hierarchy is sacrosanct. But no one escalates these situatinos to the channel head, it's like shooting yourself—or your star players—in the foot. What the hell is going on?

Since I'd taken permission directly from the senior news editor, who's liked me from day one, I'm not super-concerned. It just makes Samit look petty and irrelevant, if you ask me.

First, I mail him and copy Deepa and her assistant, saying that I'm bringing six one-hour tapes in, including the master-shot tapes; that it went fairly well, and to please book edit slots for the following three days.

Then I mail Samit, copy the senior editor, the channel head and Rahul, my anchor boss, to say that I'd asked to be sent to Mumbai to do this incredible show that I believed I was best suited to do. I add, for good measure, that I've done special shows in the past, always aiming for a certain standard with my shows, and this one has turned out above average.

I hope I've worded it politely enough. Rahul should be pleased. He keeps telling me to push for my own shows, 'take more initiative' and take more ownership of what I do. Here you go, dude!

I'm off work mode now. I go to Zenzi in Bandra to chill with a couple of friends from back in college. Preeti has let them know I'm here, and we're on a nostalgia trip. I don't do this enough in Delhi: let my hair down, drink in the day, catch up with friends. It's balm for the soul, it really is. And there's something informal and cosy about this place anyway—soon enough though, it's morning and I'm on a Kingfisher flight back home, corroded home.

5. *Whining, Bitching, Back-biting*

I get back to work, and the first thing I don't see is my boss, thank god. And I don't see my supposed protégé anywhere, either. I'm more than a little put off with her, to be honest.

Also, while I've just about started feeling ashamed of how I've dealt with the boy-toy, he's now evidently on some other trip—everyone's spotted him all over the place with a younger model. I think she looks a little like me, but I could be wrong about that. Anyway, all that public display of affection stuff, it's a little unseemly, don't you think? I mean, it's an office environment, for god's sake. I just act mature and try not to look nauseated when they're around and at it. I guess that's goodbye, then.

Samit's on three days' leave, Deepa tells me, which explains why I'm feeling so chill. That and the relief that the goss has died down pretty much. Attention has, instead, shifted to the big wedding happening this week: the man and his muse have decided to make it official it seems (he's in charge of reporters, she's in charge of editors). No one likes either too much—they both spend way too much time calling each other not just from around the world (he's quite the globe-trotter) but even from different nooks of the office building. I'm told they've been caught making out in little shady corners by young, giggly kids. What is with all this PDA stuff, all of a sudden? Of course, they're both big-enough-shots that everyone pretends to like them. No one kisses ass more than TV journos: makes you wonder how we do interviews and get you the real picture in the first place.

A couple of days go by in a pleasant haze.

And though I try to avoid weddings on principle, I go for this one—protocol, don't you know! Of course I have to mingle with all the young people there, including Neeraj naturally. I just smile genially, bolstered by the few drinks I've knocked back beforehand. A couple of us old-timers did an emergency run to the bar near office, which has pretty much become our oasis in times of need. When I say old-timers, I mean we've been around for about four (the newest guy in our group) to eight years (me and three other oldies, though none of them started anchoring like me, four years ago). Anyone will tell you that's long enough in TV to start counting your shares. Or bitching about why you don't have any. It's fairly standard practice though, the shares and the car (after what, five or six years of work) . . . Not too bad, I know. But for things to keep progressing smoothly, you need to know how to play the game: charm the right bosses, make sure they all know who you are. The usual greasing of the wheels—except here there's a peculiar feeling amongst all those who've put you on air, who aren't on air themselves, that they somehow created you, own you. Or own your image, at least, and that's the closest many of us come to reality, on a daily basis.

PRE-BREAKDOWN 75

My show airs Friday night, and I start to get some mails from within office. The news editor boss mails the entire team to say good job. Samit, who's back by now but still has not spoken to me, replies all, to say the show was well produced, and I note he says nothing about my anchoring, though a couple of other people do when they write in. I'm pretty kicked. Better than kicked, in fact. But as an aside, I'm mortified to get a call from Preeti saying I was looking great, *this* is the kind of show I should be doing, and the cleavage is a nice touch.

I don't know if it's that, or my other well-wishers, but I get the weekend prime-time special show debating urban India's attitude towards the poor. I'm on fire—I kick ass on that as well. I mean, I get the hypocrites to sound hypocritical, I get in some questions without looking like I'm giving anyone a char-grilling, and I have a great panel . . . it all just clicks.

I'm really on a roll.

Samit even smiles at me again.

No wonder I'm on top of the world. I'm sitting on the staircase, smiling to myself, when I get a whiff of the strongest cologne. I don't even have to look up to know who it is: my buddy Nikhil.

'Why are you ignoring me?' he pokes me in the shoulder and asks.

'I'm not, man,' I barely look at him. 'I've been damn busy.'

'Rubbish,' he says, green eyes twinkling. 'Come on, I've seen you busier. Let's go get a drink.'

'Ech, not today, Nikhil,' I dismiss him.

But if there's one thing about Nikhil, it's that he's a

charmer. He's known me for at least a decade, from back when I was in college, which he never lets me forget. I can't help but smile up at him; what a long way he's come since then—the biker dude with the long hair, leather jacket and all, is now looking most fetching in his suit and tie.

'What are you grinning away for, eh?' he sits down beside me on the stairs. 'Damn pleased with yourself and your show . . . feeling too cool to come out with your old buddies?'

'Ha ha, no no, silly!' He has this effect on me, I get giggly sometimes. I mean, he's bloody good looking: he used to model back in college. 'The Face' we called him, back in the day, and it's just stuck. He flirts with everyone, from the make-up girl to the weather girl, from the receptionist, to the boss's wife. We all turn a blind eye, even when it seems to cross the line a bit, because he's packing heat. He's bloody good at his job.

I'm quite in love with him myself, on one level. At least professionally. As the head of the foreign desk, technically he could sit back and let the flunkies or junior reporters do all the work except when a big story breaks; but you have to give it to him, he's totally hands-on. Even for what you and I would think are the smaller stories. Of course, it's the kick of being on air that drives him, but still.

But I manage to shake him out of my system; this is much closer than six degrees of separation. Nikhil's wife is Preeti's cousin. Of course, what's weirder is the fact that *they* hooked up way back when. 'It's nothing, M,' I remember Nikhil telling me when we met again at work all those

PRE-BREAKDOWN 77

years ago. 'Don't be senti, I was just bonking her. You know that.'

Wow, bonking. My best friend Preeti, that is. No sentiment. Not from either of them. The two of them together. And then he marries her cousin. But then again, it was much before the wedding, after all, and they were both careful and discreet enough not to let the wife know. Even now, when they meet. A veneer of civilisation hides the dysfunction within.

My phone rings, 'Hellooo,' I coo into the phone, winking at him, as I walk off, having made a plan to go out in the evening.

I'm having such a good time, I'm even ready to deal with Janki when she comes to see me the next Tuesday.

'You didn't get a chance to read my mail?' she asks, all snarky.

'What mail? I didn't get anything. I'm sorry, I've been meaning to send you a line though —' I'm much nicer than she deserves. As it is, Deepa's been giving me the lowdown on Janki. Behind that sweet exterior, is a total mover.

'I was going to work on that show you did in Mumbai,' she says, completely disingenuous now, tone changing to match mine.

'Yeah, I'd heard.' I change tone, get a bit more confrontational than usual. 'But I was already on that show, which I think you know, or knew at the time.'

'No . . . I mean . . . it wasn't like that. I just wanted to help out on the show, work with you. I'm really glad you came back, and you're okay and all.'

Here she is, her old kiss-ass self.

78 BROKEN NEWS

'And it was very nicely done,' she adds.

'Thanks, glad you liked it.' I turn to Deepa, who has walked up in the meantime, but find Janki's still standing around. 'Anything else?'

'Yeah, I mean, I wanted to sit with you. I have a meeting with Rahul, so maybe after that?'

Good for them both: he's looking for an understudy, she's looking for attention. Rahul outranks me by, well, about two ranks and a half. He's definitely a big-shot anchor dude. And bloody good at his job. I never got into protégé mode, but I'm wondering if I should have—I think he's won awards three years in a row. He's a bit of an egomaniac, but that goes with the territory around here.

'Okay, well if I'm around and free, you can let me know what you're thinking,' I tell her.

As soon as she leaves, Deepa hisses, 'What the fuck, why are you even talking to her?'

'I don't want her to think she got the better of me, man,' I say. 'I don't know, I can't explain.'

'Well, she nearly did, so be careful. She's not turned over a new leaf or whatever you're thinking.'

Janki comes back after her big meeting, and when I ask her how her story idea's coming along, she is totally blasé. Like I'm trying to hold her back.

'Well, I was thinking, with all my desk work and now the anchor training, I'm not sure I have time for stories and stuff. Unless it's a half-hour show, maybe?'

Wow, that's premature. A little prima donna she's turning into.

'Oh, well, I'm not sure if you're ready for that. I mean, you have to know how to do several stories before you

PRE-BREAKDOWN 79

can work up to a half-hour, really,' I say. 'It takes a lot of staying power.'

'Yes, but there's no point—I'd rather get on air. Rahul's told me probably in a month or two, tops. We've been going over my anchor practice tapes.'

Wow, she's certainly learned fast, I think. Rahul runs the show, and she's somehow managed to get in his good books—possibly through a clever combination of kissing ass and plain old sneakiness. And when I say sneaky, I mean slutty. Deepa tells me this is what people are talking about.

I know, I know; you shouldn't knock a sister down—but you have to admit there are a lot of women out there who will use the dirtiest tricks in the book to get ahead. No one plays fair . . . and, well, just like the hotshot national bureau correspondent said to my ex flirtatiously, over a drink, 'There are things women can do to even the playing field.' At the time, all I'd worried about was why they were having drinks in the first place, but yeah, she did sum it up nicely, I suppose.

More power to you, I tell her, in my head, and forgive her the smug look she gives me, even till today. We all make our choices, right, and Janki's made hers. Rahul's promised to make her a star, she's giving him a little something under the table—it's the oldest story in the book.

'I didn't realise you'd started anchor training? When did that happen?'

'Well, I *tried* to call you, but you didn't pick up,' she says accusingly.

'I was in Mumbai.'

'Well, they told us they're looking for an entertainment anchor and also for early morning shows. I thought that was pretty cool, so I told them I'd like to train for it.'

'Good for you.' I really have nothing further to add. I think she's figured I'm not the shit around here, when it comes to sticking her mug on air. My sympathy for her ambition has nose-dived, or is that my ego taking a hit.

It's around this time I slip up, I guess.

I mean she's still hovering around a while later, but I don't really expect her to be eavesdropping. Deepa's come back to give me some office gossip about a city reporter, and adds that this nosy reporter has jabbered something to Samit about my love life. Nothing extraordinary here, I know, but it annoys me.

So I react. And bitch out the two of them. Not the wisest move. Not with Janki around as witness, as it turns out. It wouldn't be such a big deal, if she weren't such a little cretin. I'm not even judging her for sleeping with a boss or any of that—but when she bitches me out, that's like it . . .

It's a few days before I hear about it. She's been talking me down all over the place, and I hear it from my interns. The world, I take it, thinks I confided to her that I'm at breaking point with my workload. Apparently, she's told Rahul, 'out of concern for me', that maybe on account of my heartbreak, I didn't want to be doing a news bulletin three or four times a week. Maybe she could learn to fill in? Clever plan . . . but not very practical, because she's just starting out, so it's a little *out there* for anyone to back her to replace me, you know?

And it just means I have to have a weird-ass conversation with Rahul.

PRE-BREAKDOWN 81

'Hey,' I start, pretty lamely.

'Hey, how are you?' he sounds concerned.

'Pretty good, had a great show in Mumbai, and there's a lot going on, so . . .' I smile at him.

'Great, I mean I did hear,' he lowers his voice, 'that you had a lot going on, so I was going to check in on you . . .'

'Oh, what, no no . . . nothing I can't handle,' I flash my dazzling-est smile up at him, 'though Rahul, I have been meaning to talk to you about this girl, Janki.'

'Yeah, yeah, she's doing well,' he butts in.

'No, I wanted to . . . well, this is awkward . . . but this Janki's been talking about me, I hear, with no frikkin' clue about anything, so if she says anything to you, just . . .' I pause, I don't know how much blunter I can be about something so damn ridiculous!

'C'mon M, ignore all that crap, we do what we do, you know how it is . . . people just trash-talk for no reason . . .'

Aha! I knew she was trash-talking me, the little shit.

Rahul's right though, and I smile and leave it at that. But what she can do, and has done, it turns out, is take the shine out of my image a little bit. I mean, around here, perception is everything. And people have seen us hanging around together, so they assume she has the inside scoop. And since Deepa never did manage to work Janki's lie into a conversation with Samit, there's nothing else left for me to do, really. Considering a conversation with Samit is long overdue, by this point. I barge into his cubicle.

'Hi, there's something I want to talk to you about,' I start.

He looks up at me. 'Go on, then.'

'I've heard someone is walking around telling the whole

82 BROKEN NEWS

office that I'm overworked. Which is ridiculous. Someone being this young trainee who I tried to help out.' I'm working myself into a rage. I mean, the audacity! After I tried to help her, no less!

Samit sounds weary. 'I don't even know what you're talking about. Are you feeling overworked?'

'No, of course not,' I say. 'Of course I have a lot of work to do, which I'd rather focus on, than this crap doing the rounds.'

'Okay, then get to it. Stop worrying about all this nonsense, M. I've told you before, just focus on the work at hand.'

Oh great, now I sound like an emotional, hysterical nitwit.

'I'm on my way out for a shoot in twenty,' I tell him icily. 'Just wanted to tell you to disregard whatever it is, whenever you do hear it.'

He smiles at that, and looks back at his computer.

But as I tell Deepa later, I'm not entirely sure I convinced him. Of course, to him, it sounded like I'd been trying to do damage control, *after* bitching about my workload to the juniors— and I don't even know if he's heard what I'd been saying about the city reporter and him.

I'm reminded again of how I haven't come up with a really great story idea for the longest time. Samit's seen me bust my balls over every goddamn story. It's that fire he rewarded really, ignoring some dissenting voices and promoting me out of turn last year. I want to get back to that page in his book, and you know, this isn't helping.

A week later, Deepa comes up to warn me about snatches of conversation that she heard at the stairwell,

PRE-BREAKDOWN 83

about me and the city reporter, things like 'They hate each other now', and 'This is going to be so much fun to watch'.

'They're talking about you and the bitch,' she says. 'It's not just Janki in the picture anymore.'

The reporter in question is a bit of a head case. She's gorgeous and talented and intelligent, but super-insecure. So all it takes for her to start hating me, is this one little rumour about what I may or may not have said. For the record, after hearing that *she* said I'm not wired for romance and should bag any guy who falls for the older woman routine, before I end up alone, I said the ugly slut is so far over the hill she doesn't realise that game is way overplayed, or even that *her* boyfriend is doing the rounds himself.

Now she's jumping down my throat. Thinking that I think I'm better than her. It's completely irrelevant that I might be—better than her, I mean. Who's to say what a few more years under my belt will do. But I haven't actually ever angled for her job. I hadn't even *said* anything about her being a neurotic control freak.

Try explaining that to a neurotic control freak.

In itself, it's not a big deal, but it's spilling out. She starts attacking my work. Saying I'm slipping up. On stories. On air. In pronunciation. She calls me out at meetings in front of the big guns. She does the same in front of junior, barely-out-of-college reporters. Other people join in, because it's the easiest thing to do. Pick on whoever everyone else is picking on.

'Oh, and M, our young anchor's finishing up her training next week,' Deepa informs me. She tells me someone told her that, in the new roster to be made, a young anchor

84 BROKEN NEWS

will be replacing *someone*. She says 'someone' in italics. I refuse to make myself a head-case about it, especially given my last two great shows. But when I'm off the roster three days in a row, with no real reason, it gets to me. Off-air, I don't work as well as on-air. And eventually I start wallowing in this crap, wondering what I've got myself into. Wondering if I'm past my prime professionally—if all it takes to push me over is this idiotic girl bitching me out to the right people at the right time.

Just a few short weeks later, something happens to put it all in perspective.

Real life. Or in this case, death.

My mother's younger brother dies. Half an hour before a news bulletin. At least that was when I was told. He'd been ill a while, and I hadn't seen him in years. Alzheimer's had left him debilitated by the time I was out of college, so I'm sure he wouldn't even have recognised me. But that shouldn't have stopped me from seeing him . . . it's not like he was far away—Dehradun's what, a couple of hours, max?

Just that I let my life get in the way of family visits.

You realise how cold you are, when you can hear about a death and go on to do a live show, no trace of it on your face, caked as it is with foundation and eye shadow and under-eye concealer.

Death.

Not far-off deaths, mind you, like the nameless, senseless tragedies we nevertheless try to make sense of, with penetrating questions like, 'What is the latest development in this case?' And 'What is the government doing in response?' and 'How are the families coming to terms with this _____ (insert as required from the following: tragedy, mass murder, chaos and murder, monstrous crime)?'

We've lost all sense of perspective.

Priorities, what do you say? Look at the efficient monster I've become. It's imperative the show must go on. The point is the show will always go on, just not necessarily with me in the spotlight. But that's a choice I've made.

The consequences? Here's the short list: not being there for family when they need you, relationships falling apart, friends no longer quite as tight, children growing up with a stranger . . . An uncle who saw me more on TV than off—here's someone I'm never going to see again and I can't even remember the last thing I said to him face-to-face. On the phone, yes—I'd called about my sister having a baby. And then one more time, when he told me to tell mum to call more often.

Twice in the last year, I've spoken to him. I've become hideous, in my mind's eye.

The nightmares start.

I check out. I curl up into a ball on my parents' bed. I'm no support to them as they leave for the last rites. I can't even cry, I just want to sleep. I pop a couple of pills. The same the next day. I snap at relatives who call. And then the oldest coping mechanism in the book: I go on a bender all weekend.

It doesn't help.

Makes things worse, as a matter of fact. There's the unpleasant experience of waking up in a stranger's room. I remember making sure we used protection, but I wake up with such a hammering in my head that there's no way to have a polite morning-after conversation. I don't even really remember how he picked me up at the sketchy bar. No coffee, nothing nice at his pad: really a *guy* guy, one of the young pothead types, too cool for the real world. I get the fuck out of there and head straight back to work, stopping at my place only for a shower and a change of clothes.

Work's where we go to bury our sins—a little dose of salvation.

6. Redemption Song

Office is more of a home to me than my own home. Little cubicles where we tap, tap, tap away industriously, little boxes on rosters where our names fit in nicely—there's an industriousness and neatness that's lacking from real life. And like the little gerbil I do my time, go home, do my time, go home. Before I know it, March has passed me by, the summery shimmery haze of my life turning into the sweltering cauldron all Delhiites know and detest.

I think it's mid-April actually, that we get a nasty surprise walking into work one morning.

Rahul and five mid-level long-timers have been asked to leave. They literally got into work and were unable to log on, unable to get any of their stuff together, and escorted out. What the hell?

It was a surreal scene, this is Rahul after all, the prime-time face of our channel, the face on a hundred billboards. Management's accusing him of all sorts of dirty things, from siphoning off money, to spying for a rival channel.

We don't know where to look, the rest of us. There's an eerie silence in the newsroom. We're all staring at each other, paranoid about who we've been friends with, in that

90   BROKEN NEWS

group that's just been tossed out. So much for the courage of our convictions!

I have a standard response when things turn grim: cover your ass, get out of the line of fire. So I rush out on a shoot I don't need to go on, drag out a lunch, and like most things in TV, it's blink-and-you-miss it. By the time I get back, the weirdness has kind of blown over. My story's also coming together, it feels like—I found a couple of parents distressed about the lack of safety provided to girls working at call centres, despite the drivers and cabs, and after shooting with them all day, I come back to storyboard the rest of it. It should be done by the next day—I have to re-create some crazy call centre cab driving and shoot at night to get that lonely, spooky, unsafe Delhi feeling ... and I need one girl to come on camera to say, hell yeah, things get scary around here.

Work aside, though, over the next couple of weeks, we're all looking over our shoulders. I've never seen my team so industrious. It's not just anonymous guys who'd been thrown out, after all. I can't exaggerate the Rahul effect—he'd been with us six years, and the TRPs for his weekly show were through the roof. With top ratings and star billing (primetime shows, no less) and those awards, it was very, very out of the ordinary that they even let him go.

No one I know has the real dirt, though a gazillion SMSs are doing the rounds. I check on Twitter/Facebook. Nothing.

In addition to poaching our top talent while getting huge offers from two rival channels, Rahul's supposedly fudged some of his outstation budgets.

PRE-BREAKDOWN 91

'That *can't* be the whole story, Deeps,' I say, 'unless we're talking what, lakhs? And I don't even think he's the sort, he's rich enough, for one ...'

'I think it's more than lakhs, they're saying for the past few years ... but the money, that's just one part, no?' she says. 'It's the top talent he was going to steal away; you know how serious everyone is about that kind of stuff.'

Serious, yes, but it happens *all* the time, as new channels pop up, the same people practically on rotation.

'They've cancelled leave for, like, four people, after going through everyone's email, especially all of Rahul's friends,' Deepa adds. 'And HR's called them in.'

'What are they looking for?'

'Nothing really. They found what they needed. This is just to send a message out.'

'It sounds bloody scary to me.'

'Anyway, it'll make your life easier,' Deepa laughs. 'That little Janki won't be bothering you for a while—she's no longer the flavour of the season.'

I laugh; it hadn't struck me till now. Rahul was the one who'd vouched for her, after all. Now that I make a point to notice, I see Janki scurrying around office, head down, small-faced and all teary-eyed. I give it a couple of days but that image just won't get out of my head.

I suppose it's only because I've so recently felt what it's like to have everyone on the opposite side, and because I've been obsessing about death and what kind of person I am, what I'm going to leave behind, that I chat with Janki around a week later.

Why should I be the ageing control freak who's in a twist because someone's younger, may be prettier, and is far more conniving?

Especially since she didn't win.

'Hey, how've you been?' I ask Janki. 'All okay?'

Oh that's right, central to my epiphany, she's been down and out, even before this latest blow. Barely a month or two after trying to torpedo my life, she'd been wandering around, abandoned-waif fashion. Her main squeeze, Rahul, having ditched her for a newer model.

But him being kicked out—that's the icing on the cake from hell.

She's heart-broken, I suppose, though it's possibly even worse with him out of the picture professionally too . . . anyone he's been associated with, probably getting the jaundiced eye right about now.

It looked like Janki wasn't sure what to do next. She'd been pulled off a couple of shows, but was not off-air completely just yet.

'Yeah sure,' she replies. 'Very busy. Doing much more now—you know, entertainment lives, some bulletins too . . .' she trails off. Yeah, right!

'I know, I know! I've seen you—very cool! Good stuff,' I know I sound super-corny, but I'm not lying either. I mean, it's not like super-good stuff, but she's got a certain on-screen charm, there's no denying that. Something to do with the fact that she looks a bit like Nargis.

'Hey, d'you want to get a quick cup of coffee downstairs?'

Deepa looks at me out of the corner of her eye. It's the unspoken bond: we do coffee together. Or if other people insist, we let them join us, grudgingly. What we *don't* do, except in extreme emergencies, is take other people down for coffee. I don't know why exactly, we've never discussed it. But it's just understood. Over the past year, it's only happened once. And that was Deepa's boss—extreme circumstances. Yet, here I am, shaking my head at her, even as I ask, 'Deepa, d'you want to come down? Or I'll just bring your cup up here.'

'Yeah, whatever,' she snorts.

Oh dear, not a good sign. But I'll explain later. Right now though, I just want to figure out what is going on with Janki. I want to help her get a grip. 'I don't know, I can't figure out why, exactly. I just feel you know, like, responsible for her,' I tell Deepa in my head.

'Fuck off,' she replies.

Even in my head.

'Janki, come on. A quick coffee, then. I want to talk to you about your show,' I lie.

'What did you think?' she asks cautiously, when we're downstairs. I have something of a reputation for saying what I actually think in many situations, and it hasn't made me popular, I have to say.

'Oh no, don't worry,' I say. 'Very nice. Good stuff. Just, you know, you're a little self-conscious still . . . and you need to go for an easier tone with entertainment, but that's just—'

'Yeah, I know,' she butts in, a *tad* defensive, if you ask me. She's going to need a thicker hide than that to survive here. 'I'm working on it.'

'That'll come with time,' I say. 'You looked on top of stuff, from what I saw; pretty impressive. How were the lives?'

Lives are critical to a bulletin. Some people are good at them, others not so much, but they really make or break you. It's where people get to see you interacting with real

94 BROKEN NEWS

people. It's the unscripted you—though of course you often tend to think of the clever questions beforehand. It's critical though, because as news develops, if you're caught on the back foot, you can sound like a total ass-wipe. Many of my colleagues have fallen into the airhead trap, right in front of me—and the entire country, actually!

But with breaking news, or when you're just stuck, you have the fallback questions, of course: 'What can you tell us . . .?' 'What's the latest . . .?'

'Oh, it was fine,' Janki tells me, 'except I lost the line once and didn't know how to deal with it.' Yeah, technology is always intervening to make you look like an idiot. We do live satellite uplinking, we do outdoor broadcasts, so we can see our correspondents from all corners of the country and at times across the world, but we can't do telephone lines half the time. And I've heard so many reporters tell me afterwards that, when the line did go through, they didn't even hear a word of my oh-so-clever question!

'I looked really stupid,' Janki continues. 'I fumbled on Mohan's surname . . . Srivastava . . . I don't even know what I said—just something about him being outside Bachchan's house or something.'

'Oh, that's okay. I've fumbled and stammered so many times, it's not even funny.' I don't know why I'm doing this. Why do I feel this need to reassure her? Especially after what she tried to do. She looks so fragile, I think to myself, except I already know she's not. I mean, she's anything *but* fragile. She screwed me over once, but hey, I'm nothing if not a sucker for the down-and-out.

Don't over-think this, I tell myself, I really need to get

out of my head more often. I'm doing a good deed, it's good karma, no?

But I'm not lying about the stammering bit. Oh god, how many times have I done that—tripped on my own tongue. Forgivable once in a while. I mean when you're keeping it conversational, like we're told to, it's all right, you know? But oh, the humiliation when you're stuck like an old record, stammer coming in from nowhere! B-b-b-but . . . I-I-I-let me ask you this . . . Or the worst—thoughts swallowed up by a void. We'll get you the-the-the . . . oh help! And then you train yourself to look down, break the flow, snap out of it.

'It's really just about moving on,' I'm telling her. 'You can always excuse yourself, apologise and move on. Really, acknowledging it is half the job done.'

She's not convinced.

I try and reach out a bit then, 'I heard about Rahul and —'

She lashes out at me. 'I don't know what you're talking about. He was just a boss, and now he's left.' Wow. Talk about denial. The two of them have been on the bloody grapevine forever. Even before she got her first show on air. But whatever.

'Boss, teen coffee,' I tell the guy at the counter. 'Chini kum aur accha se banaye.' This is the one refrain I've had going for two years with this dude. Not that it makes the slightest difference to him. The coffee always tastes like crap, the beans are always burnt.

But hey, you live in hope.

'So where were we—hey, are you feeling okay?' She's looking very odd. Like her face just crumpled up on her.

Oh, there I see it, what she's looking at. I see *him*. Nikhil, chatting with the pretty weather girl. WTF?! So it's not Rahul who's got Janki's heart in a bind—it's Nikhil! The resident playboy and super-smooth to boot, with that easy smile, the great hair, gorgeous eyes . . . swoon! Ask any woman in the building.

She catches my look. *Right*. She's really adding some notches to her belt.

'It's nothing,' she says. 'I mean, I haven't been sleeping well.'

Touché, I think.

But, 'Hmm,' I say, all non-committal, to the sugar I'm heaping into my cup—that is, if you can call half a sachet heaping. She takes an Equal and spoons it into her cup. Man, a lot has changed since this girl became the belle of the ball. Wow, when I think back, it was just what, almost three or four months ago that she popped up on my radar . . . trooping in, all demure and slightly rough around the edges, totally eager to please. Well, she's pleased them now, I guess, lost some five kilos already. I think someone told her she was podgy. Which she wasn't, I don't think, but TV people are insane. There's no getting around the fat debate: not with girls in general, not with TV people, like ever.

'Listen, whatever you say. If you want to talk or whatever, let me know, okay?' This is my last line, really. I'm grabbing my coffee cup to go. 'Give me a call, or something.'

'Yeah, sure,' she says. 'I should go and get ready for my next show anyway.'

She'll be fine, I tell myself. Trying to justify giving up

this conversation midway, a dead end. But wait, I can't let her get away so easily. 'Oh, and Janki,' I say.

She looks back.

'It's okay about before. I guess you thought that's just the way TV works, but don't go around back-biting people just yet.'

She's taken aback. 'I'm not sure, uh, I don't know what you're talking about,' she says, and there's just enough uncertainty to tell she doesn't quite know if I'm fucking with her.

'Yes, you do,' I say, and smile. 'Just don't try these stunts again. You're still very, very young in the business,' I tell her.

I get up, grab Deepa's coffee. It's tepid—she's not going to be thanking me for this, I know. 'God, what are you doing, trying to mentor this chit of a girl,' I can almost hear her saying. 'When you need to focus—especially now!'

She would have a point too. I mean, I'm safer now, with Janki out of the picture, but remember what I was telling you about my earlier enthusiasm and eighteen-hour days? And how Samit's picked up on my lack of drive? Talk about the need to focus.

I'm at my desk thinking about a story I want to do. I'd seen an ad on a matrimonial site Ankita's parents put her profile on. I'd told her I'd screen some of the creepy replies she gets.

But what I want to convert somehow, is this obsession with skin colour, the wheatish complexion everyone's looking for. It drives me insane. A corollary to that, I'm searching through old mails, for something an old friend had forwarded me: a before and after picture of a girl whose face was badly scarred at a very famous skin clinic in town, where she'd gone to get her skin lightened—except the euphemism is to say her skin was 'dull' and she wanted a care package to bring it back to life, or some such bull-crap.

I feel like this is something I want to do, without making it a crusade. In fact, I want to get John Abraham on this one—since he's twinkling away at all and sundry with his dimpled smile, having just done a male fairness cream ad. It drives me nuts! If we get him on board, on whatever pretext, it'll be a slam-dunk.

Picking up the phone, I ring one of the young girls I'd shot with, for some numbers.

I'm totally in the zone when my chat buddy pings me.

N: sssssup.

M: hey! workin on story

N: coolness. on what

M: fairness cream industry bastards

N: oh save the world mode?

M: nt even, patroniser!

N: no but seriously on wht?

M: not sure yet but look at the frikkin' numbers—something near ten billion rupee industry here

N: too broad story, no?

N: wht peg?

M: i'm still workin on . . . talking to young ppl . . .

N: hmm . . . I'll let u know if I can think of something

M: cool yo . . . catch u soon

N: k

I'm waiting for a college kid to get back to me with

some more numbers and I'm doodling on my pad and thinking of how this story will come together, as I know it will. I just have to pound the pavement a bit, and I'm feeling that old kick of excitement.

I'm taken out of my total absorption when my phone rings.

7. *From the Sidelines*

It's Rashmi. My one-time best office friend. That is, before she dropped off the planet with the stunt she pulled at work; her exit six months ago—around the time my life was in a tailspin—even more unglamorous than the six we just witnessed.

'The bastards. They're charging me.' Often there's not even a hello with Rashmi: she cuts right to the chase. I used to love that about her: a ballsy, grounded environment reporter.

'Because of my notice period. I refused to serve it.' Staccato pauses are unlike her, and I feel the hair on the back of my neck start to prickle.

'What happened? Why now?'

'Spineless bastards is what happened. This whole time, they said consider this unpaid leave, just figure it out and come back.' She pauses. 'And now I get a mail that I owe them fuckin' two lakh sixty grand.'

The two lakh must be because of the shares she'd have had to return, I think.

'Or a bloody legal notice,' she adds, and goes quiet.

'Babe, are you okay? Where are you?' I'm concerned

now ... she's always taken care of herself, same as me, I guess that's why we were tight.

'No. No, I'm fine,' she breathes out.

But of course she's not.

'They've taken four years of my life, and I've got nothing to show for it.'

'Hey, come on, it's not nothing. You've done such great stories ...' I taper off weakly.

She'd done her time by the time she quit. Hard-working, same as me. And now her reputation is in tatters, thanks to the creep she'd dated. Susheel, who battered her more than once in public. And yet, nothing happened to him, to *his* reputation. But we should have guessed as much. If she was their rising star at one point, *he* was the golden boy. The high-flying international correspondent, he knew the top dogs' ins and outs, from their affairs to their shady deals. He was so much a part of the system, management literally looked the other way.

It didn't hurt that his father was a top bureaucrat in the home ministry. One of our 'highly placed sources'. I didn't know that at first.

Rashmi and I'd had a couple of run-ins when he'd first started dating her. I mean, I thought he'd hit on too many of her friends, but she trusted him, and we agreed to disagree.

Me and him though? Not ever on speaking terms really. Even now, we're just about glacially cordial, when I have to do lives with him on my bulletins. We never acknowledge each other otherwise.

The first time he hit her, I suppose office had plausible deniability, they could pretend nothing had happened.

No one except two new recruits, two young guys on the input desk, were around when it happened, and she didn't tell anyone.

I didn't even hear about it till she told me two months later, in tears. I was devastated on her behalf. Also on behalf of our friendship, I have to add. It was right after another public 'incident', this time at our annual office party: at the swanky lounge bar, where everyone got drunk and all the guys, from tech support to the camerapeople to their assistants to high-flying reporters, got carte blanche to live it up, and be as sleazy as they wanted.

I left early that night, since I was going out-station for a sponsored show in Pune the very next morning. I didn't actually see anything, but the way I heard it, though, the higher-ups—from the HR boss, no less, to one of the senior editors—saw him slap her, right across the face. They saw her fall, I was told. They took her home. And sent him home too, to 'cool off'.

Management got our boss Samit to speak to her the next day. Through the glass cubicle, it was embarrassingly obvious to the whole office that *she* was being pulled up somehow. I wasn't there.

She told me later. 'It's regrettable, what happened,' Samit had said. 'But of course we're not going to let him go.'

'I was forced to just nod,' she told me aghast. 'No two ways about it ... He included *me* in their scheme. I'm complicit in the whole cover-up.'

'Of course we have had a word with him,' he'd added. 'A strict word.'

She was speechless. No comfort in his voice. The whole office staring. And the love of her life crumbling. And *she* got the warning. 'But you need to be careful as well Rashmi,' he'd said. 'Be careful, don't drink too much, stay in your senses, you know.'

'Screw this shit,' she'd said, and walked out.

Except she didn't. Didn't quite get around to that, for another few months. It broke her, I think. That she didn't stand up to them. That's what did it.

I suppose office started taking her seriously when a lawyer friend of hers got excited about suing for damages. Got her to lodge an FIR and threaten to sue the company for harassment, not to mention looking at a possible sexual harassment angle.

I guess Rashmi didn't think that they would call her bluff. Maybe she just wanted Susheel's attention again. Not realising, perhaps, that you never fuck with a media outlet, unless you have a cast-iron case. She made her threat, though, Rashmi did. She'd had enough of being voiceless. And they went after her.

They maligned her every chance they got, and you couldn't really tell who was doing it. It looked like it was just Susheel. But he had to have had help. They shredded her reputation. Made her sound like an alcoholic—and a whore. It made me sick.

'She deserved it,' I was told by someone I nearly punched out. Nothing we like moralising about more. The fallen woman.

She was painted as having fallen far off the bandwagon, her employers' magnanimity the only reason she'd been able to cling on for so long. Those were the rumours

PRE-BREAKDOWN 107

getting back to me, at my level. She wouldn't be getting a job in this industry again any time soon, it didn't look like. The system closes around its own, is one thing I've learned is *the* golden rule.

That was possibly the last straw, though I didn't know it at the time. I'd met her once in the interim: she cut herself off from us all, told me she was going to her mother's in Dharamshala. I'd tried talking to her family at first. Her mother Rupa just told me to give her some time.

'You come over whenever you want though,' her brother Saad told me, 'and don't worry, we'll take care of her.'

I didn't have time to go, as a matter of fact, life making its own priority lists.

And now this call.

'I'm just saying, I need you to help me.' She really does sound broken now, no more righteous anger. 'It's getting too much, you have to talk to him.'

To her former boss, that is, Samit. 'And say what, babe?'

'I don't know, I don't know M,' Rashmi's voice is subdued. 'I just . . . things have just gone . . . I want to come back now, M. Just tell them now, no?'

'What? Didn't you tell them you didn't want to come back?' I've never known Rashmi to be this indecisive. Except maybe when it comes to Susheel.

'I'm not mad, I want to come back, you know. It's tough . . . Just get them to agree, M.' Her voice has a nasally, insistent ring to it.

What on earth. 'I'll try,' I say. Not that Samit will listen to me, after the roller-coaster ride Rashmi's been on, but I guess it's the least I can do.

She hangs up.

108 BROKEN NEWS

I stare at the phone like it's an alien. I don't know what she wants me to do. What do I go tell Samit at this point? Should I just leave it be for a while? I'm racking my brains, a small part of me reflecting how this electronic leash is unforgiving. My focus is completely shattered. You can't ever hone in on one thing for long—if it's not your phone ringing, it's a text or an email or empty e-chatter on those social networking micro-bloggy sites. I'm exhausted keeping up with everyone's issues on every conceivable platform.

Whatever, I really have to stop getting distracted and get back to the grind. By the time I bother to check my watch, it's twenty-five minutes for my bulletin, and I've put in no work. Quickly, quickly re-write: headlines, story links. Look at the show flow. Rush upstairs to the studio, game face on.

'Hello there, you're watching the news here on —' I'm off. No time to think. Not about anything short of national and international importance. At least not for the next thirty minutes.

But it turns out to be an hour-long show—we re-roll the bulletin in the back half-hour. It's a fast-paced day, so we can't just 'chunk' it or re-play the recorded version. Another crackling day in this war-ravaged neighbourhood.

Honestly, on days like today, I don't know why I complain half the time: it's such a great job, to be a part of real-life events as they unfold on a global stage. It's enough to feel like a tiny, tiny part of something very big.

I'm feeling satisfied and fairly virtuous, when I spot Janki and a gaggle of girls hovering around Nikhil again. They're oblivious, but I roll my eyes and take a detour. I'm actually annoyed. I mean, Nikhil should figure out she's a little wet behind the ears. He's probably been playing her, and now she's going to go off the rails, for all he knows. Hmm ... not that she's exactly a virginal schoolgirl any more, not after the Rahul episode.

She's jumped on this whole thing to be a star—she and the gang of five new anchors she's hanging out with right now. They're all pretending to be friends; from where I'm standing, though, soon enough they'll be clawing each other to get the best time slots—it's quite funny actually, in a sort of soul-squashing way. The blow-dried assembly-line hairstyles, the make-up they wear as a badge, long after they have no reason not to remove it. They've fallen for their own image.

'Don't confuse yourself with what you look like on TV,' was the best advice I ever got, from an anchor years ago, shortly before she left us for an international channel. 'Don't fall for the image, don't take it personally.'

Try telling that to Janki and her new friends ... they obviously figure they'll get there faster by playing up the sex appeal. And maybe they're right. You can't really blame them: a product of the times. Results need to come in faster, sooner, and everything has to be bigger and more spectacular than ever before. So they speed up their game, sex it up. Because honestly, there are so many of us on air right now, it's hard to distinguish one from the other.

Janki for one has really pulled out all the stops. All that effort. I didn't really notice it till now, until I see her with Nikhil in the foreground: the French manicure, the coiffed TV-style hair, the plunging tanks and short skirts, the lisp, the practised-but-somehow-casual sexiness. I don't know if Janki quite realises the impact all this has. Or does she?

Of course Nikhil's no saint, he gets away with everything, and gets everyone he wants, too. Married or no.

'It's not really our business,' said Deepa, when I launch into my rant.

Deepa's tuned into me enough that she can almost foresee the need before I do: chocolate or caffeine or a cigarette. We do the Diet Coke and cigarette on the stairs. So much for quitting smoking. This past year has been the mother of all relapses.

'But what is he *thinking*. What about his wife? Why'd he bloody get married in the first place?' I'm fuming. I don't know why this enrages me, but it does. It's not just the harmless flirting.

Deepa shrugs. 'You can never tell from the outside what's really going on in anyone's relationship . . . But if you really feel that strongly about his sleeping around, you should tell Preeti at least,' she tells me.

'Well, I don't know how she'll take it. You know it's a weird situation,' I say, a little testily. Mainly because I can't articulate. I haven't been able to bring myself to tell Deepa about Preeti and Nikhil. Though I know Deepa is as discreet as they come. I just feel like it would be betraying some trust. Also, it happened so long ago.

We call it a day, and I give my brain a bit of a break over the weekend, after all that straining over problems not of my making.

8. *Inner Steel and Icy Disappointment*

Back to work mode Monday morning, and while my fairness cream crusade is partially shaping up, I'm getting no fix on Mr Abraham. I'm pondering how to pitch this without the star power, which would be a selling point in itself, the sort of stuff non-journalists lambast the media for, but you have to work with the dynamics of TV, after all. Samit thinks it's a decent idea but isn't convinced I'll pull off that particular coup.

Except, oh god, I'm pushing to the back of my mind the Rashmi crisis. I'd promised to speak to him for her, but more than that, I want to make sure to go over to her place, chat with her a bit, see if she needs money, that kind of thing. My mind's racing now; times like these, I feel I'm about to snap. I have to tell you, I've cried a couple of times in office just out of sheer exhaustion and stress.

But this is not going to be one of those days, I tell myself sternly. I have to take one thing at a time. I'm sitting on the steps, when I feel the slightest touch on my shoulder. I smile. Neeraj, I assume, for some godforsaken reason, though he's long gone from the scene.

'Why so tense?' Oh god, it's Nikhil. Smile wipes itself off.

'This is not the time,' I growl at him, over-compensating maybe, for the smile.

'Oh c'mon, you're such a grouch. Come, let me give you a neck massage,' he says. Except he says it 'mä-ssahge'— a remnant, I take it, from his England stint.

Ohhh, nice massage too. Charming. How many lovely encounters have started from one simple massage, it's relaxing as hell ... from anyone else, my mind tells me, through the haze. Snap.

I jump up and bound down the stairs, lucky not to sprain my ankle, the way I hurtle away from him.

A few hours later, a phone call, not from Abraham's secretary, but Rashmi. 'I can't, I can't deal with this ...' she's sobbing.

'What happened?' I ask. 'Rashmi, tell me!'

'No, nothing ... just wait ...' She calms down. 'He's just been so ... God, I'm such a moron.'

'What? Susheel? What? Did he hit you again?' I'm so upset the words don't come out right. 'Tell me, I'm calling the cops *right* now —'

'No, no, just ...' She's sniffling, then silent, but when she speaks again, she sounds calmer. 'No, I don't know what the fuck I'm doing. He just apologised a while ago. I mean, he sounded genuine ... and I'm just ... but now he's just left and he's not taking my calls again ... and I have to go to the clinic latest today ...'

So it turns out Susheel swung by her place with flowers and a penitent expression, and some sweet talk thrown in for good measure. Who knows why he's still hankering after her, but turns out that was enough. God, women!

PRE-BREAKDOWN 115

But of course, he flaked on her after that. Of course he did.

'I wasn't going to do it, I've been down that road, but god, I just thought . . .' she blubbers away. Didn't think, is more likely. 'We'll start again, he told me—make it work,' she says.

I can't believe she fell for this. Why would he trade in his happy life with wife—and kiddies on the way, I wouldn't be surprised—when he gets the side order to go? Why would he change? Why would she believe him? Why does she even want him back? I'm dying to ask her, to shake her out of this.

'We hung out for a couple of hours. You know how it goes, one thing led to another . . . I mean, I just can't resist him,' she went on.

Too much information, babe, I feel like saying, but this is not the time. She sounds like she's talking to herself anyway.

'And he did sound like, you know, he was so happy to meet me, and it was like old times again,' she adds. I can hear the smile in her voice. And I want to gag, because I know how this story is going to end. With her heartbroken. All over again.

'It's going to be okay,' is what I end up saying. 'You hang in there, sweetie, you hang in there,' I say, very lamely.

'Oh yeah, don't worry about me,' she says, and then it sinks in, what she said.

'What did you say about a clinic? What clinic?' I ask.

'What?' she says, her tone instantly wary.

'You said something about a clinic. Are you pregnant?' I ask, trying to keep the judgement out of my voice.

116　BROKEN NEWS

She rubbishes it with a, 'No, what rot, nothing of the sort, what is with you ... always that hyper-active imagination.'

Well, I guess I do have that. And this inbuilt paranoia about pregnancy and my friends.

'*Anyway* M,' she says, her tone a little chilly now, 'I wanted to check whether you'd spoken to Samit.'

'Oh no, not yet, I was just going to —'

'No, don't bother.' She's all business now, back to the steely Rashmi of yore, no more sniffling here. 'I might just want to take my time. Don't say anything to anyone yet.'

'Oh, sure, cool,' I blabber. 'So, I'm confused now ... did he say something about —'

She cuts me off. '—Hey, look you must be busy, I think we should talk later.' She's freezing me out. Rashmi was always good at that.

'Hey sure, okay, anytime. Talk later, then,' I sign off, breezy so she won't see that I'm a little wounded.

I don't get it, but she does sound like she's in control now, and clearly doesn't need my help, so what the hell.

How I regret that thought, that evil bloody thought.

Rashmi's story, or what I imagined of it, continues to re-play in my head. A pity, because my timing is crap: I am at the editorial meeting and not listening to a word anyone is saying. They're all here in this room, the super-boss, the medium bosses, the fancy bureau guys—with politics under their belt, they strut around, make their little speeches, their clever jokes. I assume I'm not missing much.

Except all of a sudden they're picking on our team. People are swivelling in their fancy ergonomic chairs to

PRE-BREAKDOWN 117

look at us, and I have no idea why. The moustachioed editor-in-chief with the kindly, twinkling eyes isn't looking all that kindly anymore. Silence. Is that sweat on my face? I'm about to say something stupid like 'What was that again?' when Deepa's clear voice cuts in.

'We had the right angle. In fact, the story was filed yesterday. It should have played, but the desk sat on it.'

'We didn't even know it was in, till this morning.' The rebuttal comes from a very senior desk editor.

'Three emails. And I called the desk to get them to play it.' Deepa doesn't budge.

'Why wasn't Input told? Everything's supposed to go through us—we should have been told,' says an exasperated guy from Input.

This is funny—and completely normal. It's a long-standing complaint that no one knows what anyone else is doing. It's funny, but tragic if you're a news station: you miss stuff. Which is criminal, anyway, but simply unpardonable if your reporter's already filed the story. Half the time, reporters complain, their stories are buried in the news wheel anyway—that is unless someone big enough sees the same thing in a newspaper, in which case they either commission the story as a knee-jerk reaction, or play it up, so as to say we have it too.

But when it's an original story and we beat the newspapers to it *and* then it doesn't play—well, bitterness doesn't even begin to describe it.

What's funny is the office dynamics. Pretty much everyone hates the desk, and the desk guys hate everyone right back, saying they're just a bunch of pretty boy egomaniacs who don't know their ass from their elbow.

118 BROKEN NEWS

And yet, we depend on each other, more so even than the newspaper guys. TV is nothing if not teamwork, you'll hear that everywhere; and yet, the right hand almost never knows what the left hand is doing. And certainly not what it's thinking. Which is where Input comes in, to keep track of everything—but when there's so much info coming in, no surprises that things get left out. With bureaus, and departments, and subdivisions, and of course all the politics that goes on, it's a wonder there's any streamlining or coordination at all.

Technically, that's what these meetings are for—to help us coordinate better. And then some earnest sap will put it all together and email the whole bloody lot of us, so we remember what was discussed and the rest of the channel knows what's going on too. Except by the time that's done, the entire line-up changes, the list is obsolete and we all get down to making our new lists, to show off at the next meeting.

'It's ridiculous. You can only play it once now, the story is dated,' Deepa is saying. Quite the lifesaver, considering I'm still not entirely sure what they're talking about. I figure by now that it's possibly the special report we did on a multiple-limbed baby—I had to chastise a young reporter for calling her a 'freak baby' in the script—going in for an extremely risky operation that very morning. Obviously the 'before' story couldn't run after the operation. Which is why Deepa's up in arms—and that's the gruesome pun that plays in my head with a laugh track, leaving me quite fazed.

As soon as we exit the meeting, Deepa pulls me to the side and asks, a little angrily, 'What the hell happened?

PRE-BREAKDOWN 119

You totally spaced out. You do realise they're all watching you now!'

'Watching me! Ooh, that sounds ominous.' I'm going for a laugh, but the humour's totally lost on her.

'I don't know what the fuck is going on, but you have to stop this—stop being spaced out all the bloody time.' She walks off before I can explain to her about Rashmi.

Nice.

My mood's shot to bits by now, of course, so I just flop into my chair and stare at some twenty-five mails blinking in my inbox. I'm meant to be a field reporter, goddammit, not a desk jockey.

Chat window pops up.

N: 'sup?

M: not frikkin' much. I'm so annoyed, turned into a desk jockey

N: welcome to my life

M: i'm sorry. didn't mean it like that

N: nah, no worries. i know u want more. not content to just chill like moi

M: actually it feels like that's all I do!

It's actually nice of him not to think I'm a total bitch for knocking his job profile.

N: somehow, knowing you, i totally doubt that

M: :) but I'm sick of sitting on my ass ten hours a day

N: there are worse things y'know. Aren't you working on that fairness thing?

M: It's not shaping up, and there's all this other personal stuff, friends, crises . . .

N: sounds like a lot of pressure

well I'm here if u wanna chat . . . maybe if you're free for a drink after work

M: hey thanks, i'll call you

120 BROKEN NEWS

I'm not sure that's a great idea today, when I feel like death, but I'll go with it.

N: bye babe

Dammit, my concentration is completely fucked. And I still have to plan our team's stories. You wouldn't think it, but our team works twice as hard as the bureau boys. But because they're longer-duration stories or special series and it's all in-depth, and that takes time, the rest of the world likes to look down their newsy noses at us. Shorter stories can be easier. More intense to get done, because you have to go faster, but it's a kick too. You do need slightly different skill-sets for both, but that doesn't mean there's any less friction. They think we get the glory, we think they get all the airtime. What you gonna do, that's just the way it is.

I'm in charge of planning and execution for our team. Or at least, I should be. Increasingly, these days, Deepa's been picking up the slack. It's a good thing. I'm not upset, or threatened or anything. And I suppose I'm grateful too. I mean, she is totally competent, and there's no rivalry there; as she keeps saying, I need to focus on the anchoring as well. But somehow, despite that, and even though I've pretty much been manoeuvred into this position of producer, it's still something I want to do, well, better than everyone else, and that's prickling me too—the ego's taking a hit. I think she's getting the upper hand professionally. I think that's bothering me, and I can't even tell her. She's gotten a tad more officious with me, it feels like.

Oh, I miss my old, uncluttered, glory days. Just me doing my stories, focusing on my stuff, not trying to take

PRE-BREAKDOWN 121

on more, not trying to impress Samit or anyone else, and failing miserably.

And bloody Facebook informs me how well Vikram is doing, how happy he's looking. He and his new girlfriend are all over the place. On TV, practically 24/7 between the two of them, on their new channel. And she even featured in that beauty magazine's list of twenty top young professionals to watch out for.

Asshole over-achievers. While I'm stuck, at the same position, same pay-scale as before. And the drive, where's the drive gone? God, am I burning out already?! Can't be, right? I'm barely past thirty. That's another deadline come and gone—thirty-plus as they say, and no significant other or family to head home to. My friends, now they're dropping like flies. Oh, just focus. I just have to find the energy to keep going, and hope no one notices—keep that game face on.

Less than twenty minutes later, when Nikhil swings by and suggests a drink, I surprise us both by agreeing.

9. *Emergency Dash Autopilot*

It's the desperation for a drink, to get out of office, with any company, that really has me saying yes to Nikhil—and to be fair, he's a safe zone for me, in many ways.

'What has been going on with you lately?' Nikhil asks over a cold beer. We're packed into a booth in the smoking area of one of the two decent pubs at the mall. It's very *couple*, the way it's all set up.

'Nothing, man,' I start. I don't want to say anything to this guy, of all people. 'I'm cool, it's fine.' But whether it's because of the look of genuine concern, or all that pressure getting to me, I feel my eyes well up. I hope he hasn't noticed as I surreptitiously try and wipe my tears, but of course he has.

'Hey, hey,' his voice softens. 'What's going on, babe?'

Remind me to figure out later what it is about vulnerability that gets men going. Or at least a particular kind of man: the opposite of the kind who run in the other direction as soon as they see the waterworks. Which is, to be honest, more the kind of guy I've had to deal with.

So here I am, trying to hold on to the last vestiges of my dignity—and let me tell you, it's hard. I feel like I'm unravelling. Just my luck that it has to happen here, in front of Captain Smooth.

'I can't do this. I can't . . . I don't fit, nothing's going right,' I'm babbling, blubbering away through the tears. 'It's not even Vikram, or Rashmi . . . everything's just gone to shit. I can't focus . . . I hate—'

'Shhh . . . shhh.' He's actually shushing me, this guy, trying to be all comforting. 'Don't even worry about Vikram, babe, you're above that. And Rashmi's just, well, misguided.' He goes for an endearing smile.

And that reminds me—'What the hell are you thinking? She's just a kid!'

'Who—what? What are you talking about?' He sounds surprised.

'Janki—haven't you noticed? Oh, forget it,' I say, trying to undo what I've just gone ahead and done.

'Are you insane? What the hell are you on—wait, is *that* what you're upset about?' And he ruffles my hair, eyes all crinkling as he says this, I kid you not. He does this weird melty thing with his eyes. Dude, this guy can turn it on. No wonder the chicks line up round the block.

'No, stupid,' I exhale. 'It's just . . . well, everything. All of it.'

'All of what?'

'God, Nikhil, all of it—relationships. Work. I'm sick of everyone.'

'Listen, I don't know—I've never seen you like this before. Maybe you should take a break, sort your head out . . .' He looks away for a moment.

'Anyhow, what you've done to the poor girl is terrible,' I say, suddenly tired of this sharing crap. One thing I have

PRE-BREAKDOWN 127

learned is, too much sharing, too much openness at work, leaves you screwed nine times out of ten—and those are your friends I'm talking about. That whole exploit-any-weakness is a given in this biz. I know, I know, Nikhil and I go back further than most, but you never know. So I'm ready to shut him out now: the best defence as always, is offence.

'I've not done anything to this poor girl, as you put it,' he drawls, 'that she hasn't wanted. For quite a while. I mean, come on.'

'I don't think that's any justification . . .'

But he's tuned me out, his eyes are at the door behind me and he's breaking out into a very guy smile.

Unbelievable. I turn and it's three senior colleagues trooping in for an afternoon drink. It's probably a regular thing, oh god, and given Nikhil's rep and the way they're smiling, or smirking rather, I know who they'll be whispering is his latest conquest.

I ask for the cheque. I can feel the smarmy stares burning into the back of my head. What a place: just a simple drink in the middle of the day, no more, and word will get around about what a skank you are.

So much for a quick drink under the radar. We get out of there pretty damn fast, Nikhil a little wounded that I haven't acknowledged his concern. I'm already sprinting towards my boss's cabin—before he hears about this, natch, not that I'm going to bring up the drinking. I'm entitled to my lunch break, same as anyone, right? Except I feel guilty for some reason.

'I need to talk to you.' It's a good opening line, I think.

'Okay, but I have a meeting to head to in ten,' says Samit.

128   BROKEN NEWS

'Okay . . . It's just that I'm going to need a little time off.' I can feel my voice trailing off, as I see his eyes narrow. But I've just blurted that out, without thinking, trying to play for time that I don't have. 'Not more than a couple of days, really. And I haven't had a chance to take my weekly offs over the past month, so . . .' I'm not lying about that. I've only taken like three days off in the last month—no wonder I'm cracking up!

'Yeah, okay.' He's always dismissive when you bring up days off.

'Thursday, I was thinking,' I say in a small voice.

'But I need you back on track and focused by Monday. We're meeting on the forward plan for the next season of *It's My Life*.'

So basically, I had to grovel and put up with this, just to get two days off. *And* I have to sound grateful. What a racket.

'Yeah, okay. Thanks, boss.'

'Sure.' And then he adds: 'Before you leave though, make sure Tripti's stories are ready. The big man is super-excited about this special series.'

'Okay, will do,' I say. This is not a kind man. Two stories for Tripti. By the time I'm done, it'll probably already *be* Monday. What an asshole.

I call Tripti. 'How far along are you?'

'Well, I've shot it,' she says. 'Writing my script now, should be done in an hour. So I send it to you now?'

'Yeah. Okay great, do that.' Though I have to say, an hour easily translates into two. And that's just the first story. But there's no point getting in a funk.

Right?

And this is a series I'm sure I'd love to input on—
women's issues, always up my street.

I spend the next few hours researching the PNDT Act.
I didn't even realise that in most countries it's not illegal
to find out the sex of your baby before birth. Here it's
against the law, and you can see why, but of course that's
largely unenforceable. It's ridiculous that posh, aspirational
south Delhi has among the highest rates of female foeticide
in the city—that really makes the bile rise to my throat.

These are the aunties and uncles whose homes we go to,
whose kids study with us in our schools and colleges, and
go on to inherit the world. Our challenge? Figuring out a
way to nail the hypocrisy without sounding preachy,
while making 'good TV'. Make the debate sexy, is pretty
much my brief.

I'm hoping to pitch in on this, except, I kind of missed
the boat a bit. It's pretty hard-core stuff we're talking
about and I know we assigned stories last week. My head
has been up my ass for so long, I haven't done much basic
reading at all.

Shit. Guess I should just sit on this idea, rather than
look like a slacker? Except, you can never do that when it's
a genuine idea. It practically chokes you if you don't get
it out. I look for the original email with all the story ideas.
Maybe someone's story has fallen through. Not sure, but
at least this story's not listed. I reply all, with my one-line
idea, saying I do know it's late in the day, but can we try
and add this one: a hypothetical story of a girl who'd been
allowed to grow up.

Tripti calls just then. 'Hey, my story's done. Not sure if
the stand-up fits in well, though.' I have no idea why she

insists on calling it a stand-up, when the rest of us call it a piece-to. As in a piece-to-camera. As in a PTC. It's probably just to reiterate that she got a journalism degree from some college in the States. And there, it's all so very different, as she keeps telling anyone who will listen. Yeah, and if she were any good, she'd have just been picked up there, don't you think? I know, snarky, even for me, but god, she gets my hackles up.

'Okay, I'll go through it,' I say abruptly. 'When's the second story slotted for?'

'The second!' she drawls. 'Oh, not till late next week.' She's all breezy. 'I haven't even *started* on it yet.'

Of course she hasn't. She's the queen of taking things easy till the last second. She does get everything done finally, but seriously, with the level of hand-holding that's required, I see my weekend slipping away. It's so unfair.

'Oh, well, send me some of what you have, so I can get a sense of —'

'Hey, wait, I just saw your mail.' Her tone changes. 'That's exactly the story I was planning to do.'

'Really? Wait, no, that's not what's on the list,' I clarify.

'Yeah well, that original one didn't really work, so I pitched this idea—kind of the same as yours, pretty much.'

Kind of the same? I'll bet. Not.

'I mean, unless you want to do it,' she adds in a very supercilious tone. 'Though I have started working on it.'

'You have? I thought you said you hadn't started at all, just now?' I think my jaw's clenched now.

'No, well, I have. The research. Making calls and all that.' She's totally defiant.

'Okay, fine then, go ahead.' I'm really annoyed now. But fuck it. I'm just going to let it go, be mature, take a few days off, as planned. God knows I deserve it.

And there's something to be said for taking the higher ground, right?

'God, you are *such* a pushover,' Deepa tells me later, over coffee.

Okay, so I don't know about pushover, but here's the thing: to fight for your story, on any given day, you have to want it bad enough. It's not just the one time that another reporter angles to steal your idea—it's pretty much a constant. And you're fighting at so many levels: with your boss to convince him or her it's a story; with your camera person so you both get the right feel to the story; with your editor; and then the producers who finally give it an all-clear before it goes on air. Often it's not as much your product at the end as you would've liked. So the aggression's a given, just that if you don't want it badly enough, you can't fake it. Without drive, I'm really no use as a broadcast journalist. Might as well switch to PR and save myself the trouble.

God, I need to clear my head. 'Think of a day or two off,' I tell myself. Except as is increasingly happening these days, I've said it aloud.

'What's that?' asks my work neighbour, Chandrika. Chandrika the nosy and annoying. Chandrika the judgemental. All she really does is talk about people's clothes, who's put on how much weight, how hideous they look on TV and yeah, that's pretty much it. I'm not even sure what work she does.

'Huh?'

132   BROKEN NEWS

'You just said something about time off?'

'Oh, ha ha, yeah, just talking to myself.' I hope that's a wry laugh. 'Been doing that a lot of late.' I'm trying to smile, but my face is burning on the inside—I feel like screaming.

I *am* screaming—wait, no, I'm not—but I'm feeling dizzy, my jaw's sore from the clenching and I can't focus on anything in front of me. This feels weird, but I can hold on, I know I can—just got to keep it together a little longer. Till I get home.

Tripti calls again. 'Yes?' I really can't help my tone.

'Hey, I need the script back now, are you done with it? My edit starts in like twenty minutes or so.' She's pretty brusque herself. Even though this is one of the critical points to remember when you're going on shoot: go with a rough script, so you know the sequences you're shooting. Without a clear visual sequence to match your voice-overs, your story's dead in the water. If it doesn't come together, it's a bitch to try and resurrect somehow on edit.

'I looked through it, I've added a couple of points in blue,' I tell her, as I email it. 'Let me know if you have any problems with that.'

One more mail to send, then I can get out of here. I write to the team, including my boss, telling them I'm not feeling too well so I'm heading home (a full three-and-a-half-hours before schedule) but that I will be on mail and phone blah blah. Now I've just got to get my things and get the fuck out. I don't even stop by Deepa's cubicle to say bye. I can't focus, I'm feeling really dizzy.

I make it downstairs. Out the gate. Down the road. I'm on autopilot now.

It's in this big cotton ball of grey, is when I snap. Distorted words in my head, lots of space and no conception of any time, just faces of people flying around in there, my head exploding.

Of course there's no one around to help. I've chosen this life of a recluse, somehow, after all. I drag myself up the stairs, let myself into a bare-naked apartment. I'm feeling wooden, just about manage to get my shoes off before I collapse on the bed.

That's it. Grey. Black. I'm out.

Interlude: Blackout

It's funny what happens when you snap. You would think it would be a little dramatic. Something big, like a point of reference—if not for other people, then for you—for the rest of your life. Like a signpost marking a pit-stop in a fragmented, shrapnel-strafed track.

But all the drama is in your head. Afterwards, you're simply too tired to figure it out, and during it, you're definitely not thinking. What you did, what he said, what they must've thought, how you looked, the right decision, the wrong decision, agonising, agony . . . it's all in your head.

And at this point, your head can't deal with it—no more processing.

It just stops.

It all stops.

You're exhausted beyond exhaustion. A bottomless pit, your exhaustion. A void.

You sleep.

At least, I slept. I slept through two days straight.

The third day I tired myself out walking to the kitchen and fixing myself a sandwich. So I crawled back into bed and I slept a little more.

Flat-lined.

Part 2

POST-BREAKDOWN

1. Papering the Cracks

Back at work Monday morning, it almost felt like nothing had changed, except *everything* had. I can't explain how I could just sense it—a seismic shift. Maybe on account of the forty-odd missed calls I saw first thing on Monday. You never leave your phone unattended in this business, it's professional harakiri.

'Paths are lined,' I used to joke, 'with heads on spikes of those dumb enough to think they could get away with that.' That's what I used to tell the interns and new recruits.

Not laughing so much now.

But what's bothering me more—on this day when I've managed to convince myself in the morning that the sun peeked out from behind its cumulonimbus buddies to shine for me specifically—what's bothering me more than a little bit is that thirty-eight of the forty missed calls on a weekend after I'd nearly *died* from overwork, were from office.

The other two? My mum. I'd finally gotten around to calling her this morning, before I left for office. She wasn't overly worried, she'd just assumed it was the usual work craziness.

140 BROKEN NEWS

But no one else on this entire planet cared enough about me to check in when I'd essentially checked out for two full days. Not even Ankita or Karthik. I don't blame them. I've been MIA the longest time; I started missing even our sacrosanct Sunday brunches, a *long* time ago.

What an empty fucking life. But I'm too exhausted to be depressed, it strikes me.

Zapping me back into the present now, the office meeting, where my boss Samit is totally pissed off—you can tell just by the way he's glaring at me.

'Welcome back,' he said icily first thing in the morning. 'Where were you? We were trying to get in touch.'

'I know, I'm so sorry, I had a bad case of food poisoning,' I lie calmly. There's no way I'm admitting to whatever that near-collapse was all about. 'And I didn't even look at my phone till today. I was holed up in bed all day, the past three days.' Anyone who's ever caught a stomach bug in Delhi knows this isn't too far-fetched. I'm entitled to sick leave same as the next guy, I feel like telling him. For the record, just in case you think I'm a slacker, I'll have you know, the last time I had severe gastro-enteritis, even to the point of fainting, I got my ass to work the very next day. But that was a year ago. This morning, at the meeting, Samit's making it clear with his steely gaze that I'm not out of the doghouse yet. Right then, of course, is when my phone rings.

It's Rashmi's mum. I cut the call. I can't afford to do this right now.

We start the meeting and I'm there, physically present, mentally alert, and yet I can't help looking at these people and thinking they're missing the point altogether. They're such eager beaver brown-noses, teacher's pets we'd have called them in school—only no one ever tells you that never goes away. Ass-kissers stay ass-kissers their whole life.

But anyway, so we're all here, and I look at my notebook, hunting for the points I thought I'd written down to put forward at this meeting. I was supposed to have a list of ideas ready, and I seem to have not done that at all—so I realise I'm going to have to wing it again, BS my way out of this one.

It's My Life, we're calling the series, and we're focusing not just on young achievers, but young survivors as well. Young is relative of course, and it goes without saying we'll be keeping our TRPs and target audience in mind, so we'll be using PLU survivors. People we can relate to. People quite possibly unlike *anyone* who works here, in this damn office. Most of them wouldn't know how to deal with a quest for meaning even if the monk who sold his damn Ferrari came up and offered them a bargain deal to better their souls.

One young trainee hasn't quite gotten used to this callous splitting up of society on the basis of market value. He wants to profile the rickshaw driver who's been through hell and back—he lost his wife in an accident, was told he'd never walk again, but is not only walking now, three years later, but riding as well—his will to live fuelled by his four-year-old daughter. No despair. Very uplifting and inspirational.

But it's not going down well with the boss.

'It doesn't fit this series. Maybe you can do this as a special report later on,' the boss tells him, dismissively.

142 BROKEN NEWS

'Hey, but —' I stop mid-sentence. Am I really ready to do this? They turn to look at me. It's too late now.

'I was just going to say . . . it's a universal appeal sort of story, with the baby, his baby, his motivation. Isn't that something that transcends . . . isn't that something our viewers would pick up on, identify with?' I'm actually phrasing it pretty well, I think, not lashing out at anyone, backing a decent suggestion, yes, but even more importantly, giving them a decent out.

'I don't know, let's hear some of the other ideas first,' says the boss. A little cutting, but not entirely nasty, so that's okay.

Oh wait, they're looking at me. And I have nothing. Think, think, dammit.

'We could profile that young single mother,' I'm saying, remembering a woman I had used as a case study for something else altogether.

'Surviving what? What has she survived?' The boss is being a little bitchy now, even for him.

'Well, it's not like she had a disease, I know, but socially she was cut off from her family, after the divorce. The stigma of that. She's adopted this girl, fought the system and really everyone who said she couldn't do it. It took her a while, and we could get the full picture, you know, see how things are shaping up. It's been two years or so of surviving our moral police, because she had to put up with quite a lot . . .' I trail off, but gather courage. This is *my* idea after all. 'I mean, she was slandered by her ex, it almost became a high-profile case, at one point.'

'Hmm, I'm not really feeling it,' the wank starts off. 'But okay, work on that, see if it pans out.'

POST-BREAKDOWN 143

Not quite the A-okay, but not outright dismissal either. I'm actually quite pleased with myself. Imagine what I could pull off with a little preparation!

'Anything else, you guys? Come on, we need more ideas.' He's on the ball today, really, for a change.

'Well, there's this woman who survived breast cancer twice. It had gone into remission, she got her life going again, and then it came back more aggressive than ever. She's just had a mastectomy, and you know, it's something that's getting more common in younger Indian women than ever before,' says Tripti's friend, Mala.

I've done some of these survivor stories before. There's nothing quite as gut-wrenching, and yet you leave with a sense of hope. Also an overwhelming sense of the futility of your own life. But that's not our job—to go into such things. It's to put the info out there. If you help even one person identify with another, to deal with something, that's something big in itself, right there. It's not such a bad gig, all in all.

We get a couple more ideas. There's one fantastic story we're definitely looking to kick-start the series with: a young boy who survived the horrific December 2004 tsunami—which wiped out the rest of his family. Taken in by his parents' friends in Chennai, he's now fifteen years old and besides going to school, works in rehab programmes for other orphans.

I'm happy to be part of something that showcases the human spirit; in fact, I leave the meeting feeling quite chirpy. Feeling better after a weekend I just slept through. 'I suppose it was rest I really needed,' I tell Deepa as we leave the meeting.

144   BROKEN NEWS

Except it seems I'm not going to play my usual role in this series, the boss pulls me aside to tell me. I'll be working with Deepa, he says. That's great, actually we do work well together. Just that his tone suggests I'll be reporting to her. It's never been a hierarchical thing before. But then again, she *is* a good producer, and you know how I keep saying I have too much on my plate. This is a good thing, I tell myself, as she comes up to me, smiling.

'How're you holding up? Wanna grab a quick bite?' She's trying, I know that. It can't be easy, not when I've been such a grouch.

I swear I see that, and yet, god damn the ego! 'Would love to, but you know, just have to start making some calls,' I tell her, not able to swing the politest tone. 'You carry on though, if you want.' I'm trying not to shut her out, but I can see she's hurt.

She gives a little shrug of the shoulders and walks on.

Rashmi's mum calls me again three hours later. I've been trying to reply to all those pending mails and figure out my forward plan, including the anchoring schedule. It's just been sent to me, and it turns out I have a few more late night shows than I'd planned on. Good thing I don't have a life outside work any more. All that swirls around in a haze. I'm holding on to my thoughts, or at least I'm trying to—and what she says makes no sense at first.

'Beta, I tried your number first today.' Her voice is tight.

'I'm sorry, Rupa aunty, I was in a meeting.' I try to reassure her I wasn't blowing her off. 'Are you okay? Is everything all right?'

'We're doing the ceremony tomorrow . . .' her voice

breaks. 'I didn't want the entire media to make it a tamasha, but what can I do now ...' It's impossible to make out what she's saying.

'Sorry aunty, I'm not sure what you are talking about. Are you okay? You're crying, is Rashmi there?'

But she's sobbing into the phone. 'How to tell you, beta? It's Rashmi, she, she ...'

And then the world bottoms out—she can't be saying that, she can't be. I'd just spoken to Rash what, three days ago. I just stand there stunned, as the line disconnects. It can't be.

It can't be, I keep telling myself as I dial her brother's number. 'What's going on? I just spoke to your mum ...' My voice is doing unrecognisable things.

Saad sounds matter-of-fact though. 'We tried calling you earlier. The ceremony for the last rites will be tomorrow, at noon. You come, if you can. But please also, M, tell everyone to respect the family's privacy.'

'Saad, what happened? How could this—when—what the hell happened?'

'Last night. We don't know much either, M. Just ... well, she jumped. I spoke to her in the morning—thought she'd be working late at that tabloid.'

I can barely hear him. I'd seen a brief in the city paper this morning about a young girl jumping from the eighth floor of a mall, from the terrace of a popular nightclub, but it couldn't have been Rashmi, it had to have been someone else.

This has to be an ugly, ugly mistake.

It can't be.

'Cops were all over the place. Suicide and all,' Saad goes

146 BROKEN NEWS

on bravely. 'First they thought it was an assisted suicide. The bartender remembers her with some guy, older chap. But I don't know. I don't know.'

Oh god, Rashmi. The poor family.

I can't breathe. 'Is there anything I can do? Please tell me—'

'No, M. Suno, I have to go. I'll talk to you tomorrow then. Please just make sure no cameras and shit, yaar. If you can talk to not just your office but the other bloody channels too. Ma is going to have a heart attack if one more person shows up at the door asking for reactions.'

'What! Yes, yes of course.' I hang up, stunned. Why am I surprised though—that's how we deal with death here on TV. Broadcast grieving relatives who are too shell-shocked to know that it's well within their rights to say fuck off, get your fucking cameras out of here. But the cameras will zoom in on the wailing widows or parents or bereaved children, and the reporters will go in, vultures on carrion. Even better if you get heartbreak right there on TV, prime-time material. We'll make some cooing, comforting sounds, condole with the families, the reporter will tell us that of course this is a time to be sensitive, to understand the family needs its space at this very difficult period.

And cut, you're on to the next story.

2. *Surviving Death*

I can't believe people in office don't know. . . . Or has a crew in fact been sent? I check with the city desk, but no, no one knows. Not about Rashmi. Not about Rashmi's abusive frikkin' ex. Where the fuck is he, the monster—he pushed her, he made her do this, I don't even know anything any more, but this much I'm certain of.

I go looking, in a blind rage, but no one can tell me where he is. There's nothing I can do at this point in time, but my blood is boiling, it really is. I'm going to make him pay, that smug bastard.

'M. In my office. Now,' Samit calls out, and he doesn't sound particularly pleasant.

'What is it?' I know he's heard about Rashmi and hasn't bothered to tell me. Hell, everyone covers up for everyone else here, the big boys do that incredibly well: the system shuts down to protect its own. Blanks the rest of us out.

'I'm a little concerned about you right now,' he starts.

This is unbelievable, he's going to make this about *me*?

'I can't believe it. I don't know what is going on, Samit. Why didn't you tell me? Did you know when we were having that meeting, did you already know?' I ask him, aggrieved and aggressive.

150   BROKEN NEWS

'I asked you to meet me after the meeting, remember?' he starts off, then I guess he realises he doesn't need to justify himself. 'I didn't want to say anything in front of everyone there. And there were no details, but listen, we will be observing a moment of silence in about half an hour.'

'We're shooting it?' I'm beginning to feel sick.

'Yeah. It's a sign of respect,' he starts, and then seeing the look on my face, 'Godammit, don't give me that. Of course we are going to cover this, she was one of us,' he lectures me.

'Samit, she's dead, I can't, I can't . . .' I sit down. And sit very still. That's good. Stay very, very still. Be calm.

He gives me a few minutes.

'I think you should see someone,' he tells me.

'I'm fine.'

'I'm going to ask you to go see a counsellor. She's very good.' Samit's talking to me and I can make out what he's saying but the import is lost on me. He's scribbling on a piece of paper, a number from his Blackberry.

'A counsellor?' I butt in. 'For what, exactly? Because of Rashmi's murder? Shouldn't we get the cops in instead?'

'Murder?' he snorts. 'The cops are already investigating. Listen M, I do think you should see this counsellor, and I would also advise,' his tone is chilly, 'that you don't go indulging in your usual conspiracy theories.'

I must look surprised, because he continues, 'Yeah, I know what you've been saying for a while, M. Word gets around. I know you don't like Susheel. But grow up.' He stops, the soul of sensitivity.

I say nothing, so he goes on.

'I'm sorry, really sorry it came to this, but she's been unstable for months. We told her to take a break. We'd asked her to get some help too, but she didn't. And now this . . . this drastic step. What a pity. What a waste.'

I'm staring at him, uncomprehendingly. I want to throw up, but there's nothing there. I haven't eaten all day, there's just a gallon of tepid coffee in my system.

'She wasn't unstable, Samit. I just spoke to her last week—she was looking to get back to work, she wanted to talk to you.'

He looks a little edgy. 'Well, she never called. That's not even the point. She's been having certain issues, I think you know about that—made some strong but unfounded allegations about the company. We did ask her to get help before HR took it to the next level . . .'

I'm just sitting there, stony-faced. He waits for me to say something. When I don't, he continues, 'I don't want to hear you're going around looking for Susheel, because we will not have him harassed.' He glares at me. 'He's not done anything—his reputation is pristine and beyond reproach. You need to understand that.'

'I'm looking for him because I think it was him at the club with her, and I wanted to ask him what happened.'

'No M, you will not make this your personal mission,' Samit is firm. 'He's grieving; he knew Rashmi well too, and you know it's a loss for all of us. Now I suggest you take the rest of the day off, if you want to, that is,' he adds.

'No, boss, I'm okay, I'm just . . . I want to find out what happened exactly, so if you know anything else . . .'

'I don't. Check with our crime team.'

152   BROKEN NEWS

M dismissed.

I walk off in a daze. I walk back towards him, forget what I wanted to say, and walk back to my desk. I sit around for a while, and people start stopping by. People who knew how close we were. Asking me if there's anything they can do. I ask where Susheel is, but no one knows. I call his number, he doesn't pick up. I call the operator a couple of times to connect me, and the first two times the phone rings for minutes. No reply.

I suppose it's a couple of hours, but I'm not sure— I've been busy trying to track down friends in common, most of whom are shocked, and none of whom seem to know where Susheel is—when Samit calls me again.

'That reminds me, M,' he starts off, looking at an email—I can't see from whom. 'I've been meaning to have a word with you. I don't know whether you even noticed, but we have been pretty understanding with you because of all that stuff going on last summer.'

He's referring to the break-up. Having a private personal life here is a complete farce.

'Anyway, that's not what I wanted to talk to you about. I don't think you yourself could possibily have been completely satisfied with your performance the last two months?'

'I've been doing pretty decently sir, I think. Did a couple of good stories, and started work on this new series,' I begin. 'I only took this last weekend off, after a month. To rest.'

'You got a couple of days off, yes, but, well, I've spoken to the big boss and he wants to give you some more time off,' he says.

POST-BREAKDOWN 153

'But . . . I don't *need* the time off, I need to work on our new series. And then,' and this really is the clincher, I think, 'I'm already slotted for a bunch of bulletins this week. It would throw everything off schedule.'

He's looking at me very oddly.

'Yeah, the boss said there's no problem with Janki filling in for you. She's been looking for more shows anyway, so that's not a problem. I do think you need this.'

I don't believe this. 'I *don't* need it, I don't understand why —'

He's adamant. 'This, I think, is going to prove difficult to deal with. It's okay to take time to grieve, get it out of your system. Once and for all.'

'Sir, I might take a few days, but I don't need officially sanctioned "time off" in that sense.' I don't get this sudden wave of concern. I know our team leaders sometimes really become family, often times, in fact. But it's never happened with Samit and me. With the news editor boss, maybe, he used to keep telling me I reminded him of his glory days. But if it was him, then surely he'd have told me himself?

Samit tires of arguing with me. 'All right, all right, if you're going to be this way—go see the counsellor on our panel. I'll have a follow-up discussion with her. But today. Call her today.' He's emphatic as he hands me the number he never got around to giving me earlier. 'And today, you take the rest of the day off. No discussion.'

I walk out, trying to make sense of what's going on, none of it really sinking in. It can't just be concern. There are other friends of Rashmi's around, I can see a couple of them.

154 BROKEN NEWS

Unless they think that I'm going to cause trouble somehow—it hits me in the face. They're quarantining me. But what is it they're looking to hide? Susheel's involvement? Has he confessed to them? What the hell should I do? Isn't there anyone who can help? I'm so bloody confused, my brain is reeling.

Nikhil sees me before I see him. He's taking me to the staircase for a smoke before I even register his concern.

He's already heard.

'Are you okay?' he asks.

'No, of course not. I just heard about Rashmi.' Nikhil and Rashmi had been good friends too, but you can't tell by looking at him—no reaction. 'When did you hear?'

'I got a call this morning.'

'Thanks for telling me. I heard from her mum.' I'm actually more pissed off than ever. They bothered to call him, the golden boy, and no one, not even he, thought to let me know.

'Listen, I wanted to call you, but I was in shock,' he says. 'And I figured you'd have heard. It's horrible, horrible.'

'Yeah.' I take a long drag.

'I wanted to talk to you, M,' he says, 'and about something else too . . . um, they're a little concerned about you.'

'Why?'

'Well, you know, you made that fuss the last time, with Susheel,' he says, reminding me how I once made a scene in office, demanding action be taken against Susheel after the big party where he hit Rashmi. I'm glad I hadn't just sat around and twiddled my thumbs like this dickwad. But he's going on. 'They're just worried, I guess. Not just about that and how you're going to react, but also, you know, it could get embarrassing . . .' He doesn't finish the thought.

'It could get embarrassing for who?' I ask him, but there's no reply. 'Someone is dead, Nikhil, what the hell sort of embarrassment are they worrying about?'

'I know, I know,' he sighs.

'Nikhil, I can't believe how ridiculous all this shit is. They're asking me to take time off or go see a counsellor or some shit . . .' As I'm telling him, he's nodding.

He knows already. Of course he does. Bloody typical: they make a decision on your behalf and the rest of the world hears about it first.

'You know, that's not such a bad idea. You were sounding so off the other day, and now this —'

'I was not,' I break in, and then it hits me. 'What the hell—did *you* tell them? What I told you? I was just venting, for fuck's sake, man.'

'No, it's not, it's not like that,' he says, very lamely. 'M, I'm worried about you. Samit was asking me what I think about how you're coping and stuff, and I was, like, you know, I think she's fine and all, and, well, a break isn't the worst idea.'

'You asshole, that was just me *venting*. How the hell do they think I'm going to cope—and anyway I didn't even *know* till like two hours ago?'

'I think, uh, um that is to say . . . I think Susheel said he was concerned that a couple of people here would get after him—and he blames himself as well, you know, he loved her.'

My ass. The bastard.

Nikhil goes on, 'The bosses are a little worried about,

you know, how he's going to deal with this as well . . .' He stops.

I'm furious at him. Furious. But I can deal with him later. Right now I just need to use him to get some bloody info. So Susheel is concerned about me. He's screening my calls, the little shit, and he's got the bosses doing his dirty work for him. Bastards.

I change tactics.

'Where is Susheel? How *is* he dealing?' I hope to god my tone sounds sincere enough, because inside I'm just waiting for that mother-fucker to show himself. 'C'mon, you can tell me,' I nod at him like he's a five-year-old. '*Of course* I'm upset, who wouldn't be?'

I pause to let it all sink in. 'You know, it's a good thing they're giving me some time, really. I have to go and see if I can help Saad and Rupa aunty.'

See, I can sound reasonable.

'Um . . . well, I'm not sure I'm supposed to . . .'

'Nikhil, c'mon man, you know me better than them,' I appeal to his ego; it's never let me down in the past. 'Give me a little credit here. It's a huge thing, it's a huge loss for all of us, man, Susheel included.'

'Well, yeah, you know, he's devastated, but hanging in there.' Nikhil says. 'He's in town, but just not at home, he's staying with one of our . . . well, he's staying at my house actually. I volunteered to help out, so, you know, people can't get to him.'

People.

Like other reporters.

People within our office. People from outside. People who gave a shit about Rashmi. The cops. Those kind of people.

POST-BREAKDOWN 157

Man, hiding him away—these guys are good.

'Well, I'm sure you'll take good care of him.' I give him my fakest, sweetest smile.

'Well, you know, Ruchi is trying to help out,' he says, referring to the wife he cheats on regularly. 'He's devastated, man, bloody devastated,' he repeats.

'Yeah, I'm sure.' My tone slips a bit. 'I cannot even imagine.

'So, Nikhil,' I allow my voice to break, 'did he tell you—I mean, he was with her last night—what happened?'

'No, he wasn't with—I don't think . . . Wait, who told you that?' Nikhil trying to play the world. But I'm done with that whole game, and I'm going to get the info out here, if it kills me.

'Oh, I heard, actually. The cops were looking for him too, no? Because they were arguing at the bar.' A little embellishment never hurt.

'Well, I don't know about arguing. I mean, the cops spoke to him, took his statement. And I think they're coming to office later today too, to question . . .' He stops mid-thought.

Wait a second. Wait a frikkin' second. They're not quarantining me to make sure I don't talk to anyone else in the company. It's the cops they're worried about.

'Oh, right. Of course, to take statements and stuff,' I try and make it sound innocuous. The Face, he may be, but he's not dumb.

'Hey listen, M.' He's shitting his pants, I can tell. 'I wasn't supposed to tell you any of this, you have to—you can't—I mean, it's all off-the-record, you know? You can't tell.' He's pretty bloody nervous now.

158 BROKEN NEWS

'Of course I won't, don't worry, don't worry.' I'm patting him on his shoulder. Ech. 'So anyway, I should probably get going soon.' I almost laugh, he's looking so relieved. 'When are they coming again?'

'Oh, after lunch, like an hour or so, they'd said. You have time, don't worry,' he says. The jackass, he has no frikkin' clue.

'I'm off then.' I get up to go. He's still looking pensive, that look on his face like he may just have said too much.

Yeah, I get that a lot. I'm a reporter, remember. These guys have no idea what's going to hit them.

I suddenly remember that I'd spoken to Rashmi last here, standing on these stairs. I push the thought away. I can't think about her . . . about it just yet. Right now, I have to find Mohan, our crime reporter—he's the right guy to talk to.

3. *Planning His Downfall*

I avoid meeting anyone's gaze as I walk over to the crime desk. I hope Mohan is there. He's a young, ambitious guy I've hung out with a bit over the past year—he's pretty solid. Better not to let him know that they're asking me to make myself scarce for a bit though. He's on the phone, so I plonk down on the seat next to him and try and keep my face impassive.

He hangs up. 'Hey, what's up?'

'Not such good news. You heard about Rashmi?' I start off.

'Yeah, it's really tragic. I know she was your friend— are you okay?' He sounds genuinely concerned.

'Yeah, not so good . . . have to go and see her family, see how they're coping. Just wanted to check with you— where are the cops taking the statements?'

'Oh, actually they're already almost done, I think. One of my guys at the police station called me a while ago, said he'd be out of here soon—oh shit, were you going to make a statement?'

'Yes but I got stuck in a meeting, didn't even realise the time. Can you call and check if they've left, by any chance?'

162 BROKEN NEWS

'Sure, hold on.'

He dials a number, rattles off a couple of lines in Hindi—I'm not even trying to follow the conversation.

'Hey, they haven't left yet, they're taking a statement from Samit, downstairs in the meeting room. I think after that, they'll wrap up.'

. I think I'm going to need some moral support.

'Would you come with me? I don't want to go alone . . .' If I ever needed to play the vulnerable card, it's right now—and I do genuinely need him.

'Sure, sure, give me five minutes. God, are you okay? Do you want me to drop you home after or something? I don't have a shoot today at all, so let me know.'

'Hey thanks, I might just take you up on that.' I'm touched; this twenty-five-year-old is the only one to have shown this much emotion and concern all day.

We head down to the meeting room. I don't want Samit to see, so I tell Mohan I'm going to sit in the free office space next door. He's adorable . . . thinks it's because I'm all shaken up. He's still being all supportive—younger men, what can I say. He goes out to find out when they'll be free to see me and is back in seven-and-a-half minutes. That's right, I'm counting. I have nothing better to do— except clear my thoughts, and figure out what exactly I'm going to say to them.

He comes back looking a little perplexed. 'Um, your name's not on their list, they tell me. Are you sure you're supposed to give a statement?'

'Well, I spoke to her just a few days ago, doesn't that help the case?' I ask, innocently.

'Yeah, okay, come on, I'll take you in—the guy knows

me.' It's a station house officer who's doing the interrogation because the case is sensitive, Mohan tells me.

I follow Mohan in. And I have figured it out, a way to nail the bastard without actually seeming biased. I'm glad that Mohan's coming in with me—not sure that's quite kosher, but then again, nor is what I'm doing, not in the least.

The SHO sits me down. 'Ma'am, good morning. Tell me, Mohan says you knew the deceased well.'

The deceased.

Just like that.

'Yes, sir, I spoke to her just a few days ago, so I'm not entirely sure . . . well, let me just tell you what she told me.'

'Yes, go ahead.'

'I'm not sure about this suicide thing . . . but she was upset a couple of weeks ago, as you must've heard from the other office people.' He nods, so I get to the point. 'But when she spoke to me—it was Wednesday or Thursday, I'm not entirely sure—she was much calmer. Wanted to talk to the boss about coming back to work.' I make sure to talk slowly and clearly. It actually helps me not deal with the fact that Rashmi's a 'deceased' now.

Then I throw it in, casual-like. 'And also because she'd made up with Susheel.'

'Made up with Susheel?' He looks down at his file, looks at a list of names, I'm sure of it.

And now to navigate the waters I'm stirring up.

'Oh yes,' I say, all innocence. 'Her boyfriend, Susheel—he works with us, you know,' I'm trying desperately to sound nonchalant.

164   BROKEN NEWS

'So it's a difficult situation, of course. I think they had an argument the night of the accident . . .' I refuse to call it a suicide. I hope I'm being vague but clear enough to get the point across.

'Who told you he was there with her on the night? You were present?'

'Oh, no sir, no, I wasn't. But I must've read it in the newspaper that there was a male friend present, so I just guessed . . .' I start, and then go for it. 'Oh no, that's right, we just assumed it was him. I mean, I was talking to her brother and he said her friend was with her, something about an argument.

'I don't know what they actually fought about. But sir, I mean, he is married, I don't think they could have gone ahead with things, despite the baby and all . . . she had to have the . . . operation.' I can't say abortion, and this is guesswork on my part, now. I can feel Mohan staring at me, and I force myself not to look at him.

There's complete silence. I might just have blown it, misrepresenting the facts. Do these guys have access to actual phone conversations? They might listen to recordings, if they do? Because then I'm screwed, they'll find out I didn't actually know for a fact that she was pregnant and had an abortion. Can I be booked for implicating someone without evidence? Or am I just getting paranoid again?

I'm assuming Susheel was at the scene of the crime, of course; who else would she have been arguing with before she died? Susheel, the bastard, getting away with his massive cover-up.

The cop looks pensive. 'No one else has mentioned this

baby with Susheel,' he says a trifle accusingly, giving me the once-over, and then looking over at Mohan.

I don't want to involve Mohan more than I have already, so I answer before he can say anything. 'Well, sir, I don't know if she told anyone else at all.' I stop to gather myself, and then plough on. 'She called me before she had to go to the clinic,' that much at least is a fact.

He can't dismiss this information now. I'm obviously a reliable source, I know the family, and clearly know enough about what Rashmi was going through.

'We'll look into this,' he says gruffly.

We're done with the statement. They take my contact details, and let me know they'll be in touch if they need more.

I hope they nail the son of a bitch.

And only then do I truly realise what I've done.

I'm quite possibly going to lose my job when they find out. There's nothing else for it though, but to put up a brave front. And ideally not tell anyone in office. Only problem with that little scenario is, I'm going to need someone to get me all the dope they can, on Susheel, on management, on the cover-up.

And it can't be poor Mohan, I don't want anything to happen to him. He might already be in trouble, I think, and feel terrible for exploiting his innocence and warmth. I thank him and say I'm going to get my stuff and get out of there. All true.

I just make one call first.

'Are you mad! What were you thinking?' Deepa shrieks at me. We're at the little café down the road.

'Didn't you hear a word I said?' I'm a little wounded, but

166   BROKEN NEWS

I really need her on my side at this point. I have to convince her—there's no other way. I didn't know who else to talk to. She's the only one I think who gets the whole picture, who gets me as well. 'He's got something to do with it, and I have to make sure they at least ask him some tough questions.'

'Do you think he *murdered* her?' Deepa asks me after a few seconds.

'I don't know, no, I guess not, but he's complicit in something. He knows more than anyone thinks, and *he was there*, goddamit. He's responsible.' I'm speaking too loudly now and people are giving us funny looks.

I try and calm down.

'The problem is,' I exhale, 'they're not taking this seriously enough. These fuckers are on his side. They always thought she was a nutcase, they don't give a shit.'

'I understand.' She's looking concerned, but wary. I don't think she wants me to flare up again. 'But listen, M, you have to understand from what Samit told you, they specifically did *not* want you to interfere.'

'I know, I know, that's why I was so sneaky about the whole thing.' Hopefully by the time he hears about it, I'll have figured out a credible excuse, to bullshit my way out of it.

She looks tired now—of what, me? Of worrying about me? Worrying about taking the rap? But I don't acknowledge I've put her on the spot. I need her to keep a lookout when I'm not around in office.

'Babe, I'm going to play this their way. I'll make an appointment with the office-appointed counsellor, that's not a problem—I'll do that. I'm just saying that when I'm gone, if something comes up, will you let me know?'

POST-BREAKDOWN **167**

She's not following, I can tell from her face. 'In terms of the investigation?' she asks.

'No, not so much that—more in terms of what's happening around office. What people are saying. If Susheel comes back with, you know, an axe to grind. What management says about the whole thing, what goes down.'

I think I've covered all bases. But even though she's my friend, I know I have to make sure not to overplay my hand, not to sound too desperate.

'Yeah, sure,' she says.

'Just so I know what I'm walking back into,' I clarify. 'I don't know whether I'm going to have to take that break or not.'

Silence for a moment.

'Well, I should be heading back now, I'm going to miss the drop,' Deepa says.

I can see she's upset with me.

'Are you okay?' I ask, trying to sound concerned, though really I can't think beyond Rashmi and the mess I'm trying to sort out. I have to go for the last rites tomorrow, and it hasn't fully sunk in that I'm never going to see Rashmi again. That just seems beyond comprehension.

'Yeah, yeah, it's just . . . a lot to digest,' she says. Perfectly justified too—I'm asking her to take my side, after all.

'Okay, well, I'll see you soon then, take care, you.' I'm well aware that she's one of the few real friends I have left at work. I should reach out somehow, hold on to her. But it's a weird space I'm in these days. In charge of very little, in control of very little—not even my own fuckin' head.

168 BROKEN NEWS

Time to get going. I head home, and then give the shrink a call. No answer. I send a text, a polite one saying I'm from this channel and have been asked to get an appointment.

There's so much to do. To keep track of the police investigation is one thing—I'm going to need Mohan's help for that. I send him a sweet text thanking him for his help today. I also have to get to the cremation ground for Rashmi tomorrow—there's no one to help me with that though.

This is really what I hate about being single. You're left in the lurch when life comes calling. When you really need someone else to be there, you have to go it alone. There's no one on the horizon, and my friends are long gone. I can't even blame them, I mean I've let everyone down over the years. I've let myself down.

And then I realise how selfish and whiney I've become. Rashmi had reached out to me for help, and I'd done nothing. If I'd spoken to Samit, or tracked down Susheel maybe . . . maybe . . . this is where it finally catches up with me.

I'm sitting there crying now, sobs that wrack my entire body—and yet I have the distinct impression that I'm outside, watching myself bawling away. No wonder Samit thinks I need counselling. This isn't exactly true of course, he has no idea how badly I am in need of therapy—he's just trying to make sure I'm still a worth-while employee, up to a minimal level of competence.

I'm not though. Not by a long shot. I'm exhausted again, beyond belief. The best way to deal, I realise, is to just sleep on it. Avoidance—the oldest trick in the book.

POST-BREAKDOWN 169

I wake up a little past midnight, starving, but otherwise curiously empty. How will I handle the last rites tomorrow? I have no idea. How am I going to help Rashmi's family? Maybe I just don't have it in me, a small voice says— maybe not.

Maybe you do, Rashmi's voice seems to call back.

4. Day of Mourning

I'm up ridiculously early, by my standards—six in the morning, no less. And I don't know quite what to do with myself. I start cleaning up the place. It's become such a pigsty, it's not even funny. I have to call my mum at some point, I realise: she might be able to help me. I sit on that idea. Sweeping, mopping, doing the dishes and then I should wash some clothes. I still haven't hooked up the washing machine, but there's something about the physical labour that helps—sweats some of the stress out of my system. I plug in my iPod, blast The Verve, which for some reason today just reminds me how alone I am. Pathetically and desperately so. Funny, how it all comes back to that.

By now it's about 7.30—I think it's safe to call.

'Hi mum, what you up to?'

'Hi M, what a pleasant surprise! Just the usual, having a cup of tea and reading the papers. Dad's getting ready—'

And that's all it takes really.

I start crying. 'Mum, it's ... Rashmi. She's ... she's dead.'

'What!' Mum hadn't met Rashmi more than the once,

174 BROKEN NEWS

but she's seen her on air often enough, and I've told her the back-story before.

'Yeah, they're saying she killed herself—I don't know, Ma.' I'm quite inarticulate by now. 'Do you think you can come with me? To the cremation? I don't know how to face her Ma . . .'

There's a slight pause. They're so used to my being militantly independent, not asking for anything, not even their time.

'Of course, baby . . . listen, why don't you come home for a bit?' That's all she has to say, and I'm packing my overnight bag. No one else can make me feel better, the way she can, sometimes.

I get a call. It's the counsellor. I tell her I'm a little tied up today, but can fix up for the next day—unless she's free this evening. She's not, it turns out. But what the hell, I might as well take the time off if they're forcing it down my throat. I don't see myself making it work, at office, not today, at least.

I text my boss to tell him I've fixed up an appointment with the counsellor the next day, so can I come into work after that. *'Fine, see you then'*, is the reply. The hide of an ox, that man has.

I shower and change, grab my bag and am out of the house. And of course have to go right back up the stairs, because I've forgotten my phone and car keys. And then I'm worrying if I need to stop at the ATM, do I have enough money for the counsellor on me for tomorrow. It's ridiculous, I shouldn't even be thinking about money. But the thing is, I can only think of the most mundane things, or I'm going to fall apart. It takes all my concentration to

POST-BREAKDOWN   175

do that—wrap my mind around every tiny little thing, because the rest of it is too big, too daunting, too bloody depressing.

It takes me just about twenty-five minutes to reach my parents' place. And yet, I haven't been since forever . . . since the last crisis. I think they know they're my refuge, you know? Mum just gives me a giant hug and sits me down with a big mug of tea, just the way I like it.

'When did it happen? It's terrible, just terrible —'

'I know Ma, I know. I can't believe it. I just spoke to her a few days ago, and now . . .' I shake my head. 'It looks like she killed herself. I think her no-good boyfriend had something to do with it. I mean, I *think* she was pregnant . . . it's what she hinted at when we spoke.'

'Oh, that married man. Why you girls pick these types—'

'Ma, this isn't the time, please, come on!'

Our generation doesn't 'get' it. We make lousy choices. We do stupid things. And then we do even stupider things to get out of the stupid messes we find ourselves in. I've heard variations of this before, and I don't want to get into how I think it's her generation that's to blame—they spawned us after all, insecurities and life warts and all.

'No, you're right. I'm sorry, I'm just so upset. What are they saying at work?'

Now this is one of those moments where you either say it all and get it off your chest, or you just don't, out of concern for the parents and how they'll take it. Or because you're an emotional cripple, which I'm beginning to realise I am.

With Rashmi, I think I shut her out when I should have

176   BROKEN NEWS

pushed a little harder, pushed through, for the sake of not just our friendship, but for her. I mean, maybe I could've prevented her from taking this stupid, stupid, meaningless, rash, ridiculous decision . . . I didn't realise I'd said half of this out loud, till I felt the tears and snot streaming down my face.

'Baby, there's probably nothing you could've done in the first place. If she wanted to let you in, I know you'd have done something.' My mum's so positive I could have helped, so confident that I didn't fuck up. 'It's just one of those things. You don't know what's going on inside someone else's head—almost never.'

I sniffle. That reminds me, I need her help. 'Her brother said I should come around noon. I don't even know what to do, what to wear.'

'Don't worry, I'll get something out. Why don't you just lie down, take a nap till it's time to go. I'll call my cab guys to take us. Where is this?'

'Near Nizamuddin—the Lodhi Road place. That's where the cremation is happening . . .'

'Okay don't worry, I know where it is. Go now, take a bit of a nap.'

A nap it is. I'm exhausted after all.

'I'm worried about her—she looks terrible. What do we do?' I wake up to hear my mum whispering into the phone. I wonder who she's talking about.

Oh. Riiight.

It's not like I don't feel okay. I have a moment of clarity as I wake up. It hits me that you're not in charge of your life after all. Or your death, as the case may be. You think you are, because we all make these stupid little rules to

POST-BREAKDOWN   177

live by, we have our little ways of doing things, our set habits, as we try not to fall through the cracks that are looming larger and larger till they're crevasses that swallow us whole.

And whoops, there it is, your life is over—and you don't even know it. I wonder if it's a relief. Day to day to day can be overwhelming, often enough.

My mum's giving me a funny look, so I give her a reassuring smile. 'Don't worry Ma, I'm not going to off myself, in solidarity or anything.' It's meant to be funny but it totally falls flat.

'That's a terrible thing to say. Terrible. I'm just concerned about you, that's all.' Mum's not a fan of gallows humour.

We leave together within half an hour.

You know, it's funny, I don't remember much about the last rites ceremony at all. We got there, I saw Saad and Rupa aunty, and we went over and all of a sudden, it felt like I was underwater the whole time—underwater and suffocating. No Rashmi. Ever again. I followed mum around and then had a panic attack, I had to get out, all those people—the family looking stoic, people from office looking sorrowful, which made me want to scream, they did nothing when she was alive—suddenly, I couldn't take it any more. I asked Mum to get me out of there in twenty minutes flat. Bad karma, I'm sure. But Rashmi would've understood.

'What are they saying at the office?' she asked me on the way back home.

'Good question.' I want to call Deepa, but the deal was she'd call me. I should just wait.

I tell her instead that they've given me a day or two

off—that I have to see a counsellor. She's not too pleased about that.

'Why? Do they think you're in danger? In trouble?'

This is middle-class India. We don't do counsellors. We don't do therapy. Which is why it's a big deal the office is sending me to a counsellor. It's almost like a way for them to get to the next step and get rid of me, altogether— or is that just my paranoia coming through front and centre. I don't know, though I can tell you no one talks about therapy openly. Ever. I do know one thing though. I'm going to ride this out, and then take a long, hard look at what I'm doing with my life.

'No Ma, I guess it's just standard protocol,' I try and reassure her, as we pull into the house.

'I heard about your friend. I'm sorry. It's rough,' my dad says when he gets home from work.

'Yeah, I know, thanks though,' I say. I look up to catch a look between them.

'*Whaaat*? I'm fine!' I snap.

'They're asking her to see a counsellor,' my mother tells him.

'What for?!' We're not really into self-realisation around here, but even I'm caught off-guard by the aggression.

'I don't know. Maybe they're worried because we were friends. Plus they're scared I'll say something about her no-good boyfriend.'

'What, that married creep?' Dad's up to speed on pretty much everyone I work with. He asks about them every so often, the people behind the war-paint as he calls it, though it's not like he thinks any of them are better than two-bit actors, half the time. But he does stay glued to all the breaking news, as far as I can tell.

POST-BREAKDOWN   179

'Yeah. Well, I think it is a bit much, making me go—but I don't have a choice, so I'll go and play nice with the counsellor. And then get back to work tomorrow.'

'Don't worry, I'm sure it will be fine.' My mother's reassuring one of us, I'm not entirely sure who.

'You don't worry. There's nothing wrong with me,' I tell her. 'And if there were, I wouldn't be spilling it to an office-appointed shrink, that's for sure.'

'Just say what you think they want you to say—you're good at that.' Dad's always got the right attitude—practical advice. And he's right too. I really can't afford to tell the counsellor anything the office can use against me. She's on their side, after all. So I won't bring up Susheel or anything about the cover-up by the big boys. I feel like something is dying inside me: I'm not sure I have the strength to fight this fight.

'Okay, well, I'm just going to lie down for a bit, listen to some music. Wake me up for dinner,' I tell them. I can't remember the last hot meal I've had, as a matter of fact, but there are some things you don't tell your parents, especially not when you're past thirty and pretending to be a functional adult.

5. *Shrink-wrapped*

I wake up a few hours later—it's past ten o'clock and I think Dad's passed out in the guest room, because of course I was hogging the master bedroom. Mum's still pottering around, and she's pleased I'm awake because she's made her famous chicken curry.

'I'm going to be out of here tomorrow pretty early, around nine—your dad too,' Mum says. 'What time do you have to go see the doctor?' It's quite cute, I think, denial on both sides of the genetic divide. I guess doctor sounds more innocuous than counsellor. More respectable.

'She said to come in by twelve,' I reply. No point trying to fight her on terminology. 'I figure I'll go in, chat with her and then get to work.'

This is my mother, so of course she's not fooled by my bravado. But she plays along. 'Okay then, but let me know if anything goes wrong, if you want help or . . . you know I can just send one of the boys to pick you up, if you're not up to driving, darling.'

Her boys, her taxi boys—they're all fond of her, she tips very well and is quite the regular. One of them is a millionaire, she tells me. He sold his family land on the outskirts of Gurgaon for a huge amount—retail realty, the

184 BROKEN NEWS

next boom—but he drives around for fun and because his friends work at the stand.

'Don't worry, Mum. I'll be fine tomorrow. But if anything comes up, I'll give you a call.'

'I'm sorry I can't come with you tomorrow. There's this big meeting with the board at the company, but if you want me to try and shift it around —'

'No, no, don't be silly Ma, I'm going to be fine! But thanks for today, really—I don't think I could have done it without you . . .' I'm not kidding, either. Something about knowing she was there made it easier to deal with.

'Okay . . . well, have some breakfast and go. I went to Khan and picked up some ham and salami for you. And I'll pack some food you can carry with you.' Oh, I love the way mothers worry about food and how they think it can make everything okay again. Maybe it works, I don't know; I do know it's her way of showing me she loves me. And maybe it's that which prompts the outburst. All of a sudden the two of us are crying. I'm sobbing, she's holding me and it all comes pouring out—the hurt, the anger, the disbelief.

She puts me to bed like the old days, tucks me in with a kiss on the cheek and the promise that things will be all right in the morning.

I don't know why, but suddenly I'm exhausted again, waves of emptiness beating against me from the inside, and it's that emptiness I'm looking for—the release. God, you'd think *I* was dying.

I sleep. Again.

When I wake up, the flat is empty. They've left for work. I get myself something to eat, check my mail, more

out of reflex than anything else, reach for my cell phone—
wow, no calls. I guess I'm really not Miss Popularity at
office any more.

Damn battery is low too. Of course I haven't brought
my charger either.

But priorities . . . I have to focus on making it for the
appointment in Greater Kailash I. It's already ten. I figure
I'll get there by eleven or half past that and take it from
there. I don't know what I'm going to say. Just that I need
a clean bill of health. I'm a little nervous about, well,
losing my job. I know I'll find another one, but once
you're burned in the media, word gets around pretty damn
fast. Especially if people think you're not quite right in the
head. I try to stop my stomach churning. I'll be fine,
right—I've weathered all kinds of storms before.

Not this kind, the voice in my head says.

I get late getting out of the house, especially because I'd
forgotten about that damn BRT corridor in the middle of
the city—traffic not moving for an hour. That's just great,
I'll make such a wonderful impression on the counsellor.
But it turns out not to matter. The counsellor's previous
appointment eats into my time, so I get a chance to catch
my breath. The waiting room is nice too, magazines,
potted plants, and best of all, enough light. Feng shui-
approved I'm sure—it's that kind of place.

When she finally meets me, Dr Sharma is a surprise. I'm
expecting someone older; she looks not a day over thirty-
five, and I'm not sure that's a good thing. But her degrees
on the wall show her to be a psychologist with a doctorate,
that too from the University of London, so I'm sure she's
qualified and all.

186   BROKEN NEWS

'M. Hi, take a seat. Right over there is fine.' She's got a soothing voice, but there's something about her face that reminds me what I'm here for.

'Hi Dr Sharma, thanks for agreeing to see me at such short notice. I'm supposed to get some sort of evaluation done, for work. How do we start?'

I'm trying to be no-nonsense about it all, but I wonder if she can sense the fear under the surface and somehow know that I'm not entirely a hundred per cent there. They have a talent for that, these head doctors.

Shit, this stuff is getting to me, I can tell you.

'Why don't you just start by telling me why you think they've sent you here, to me.' She manages to say this without sounding judgemental at all, which is nice.

'Well, I'm not sure whether it's because . . . well, to be honest, I think it's because of my friend Rashmi. She'd been out of it for a while—unhappy at work too, and well, she was . . . well, she's just killed herself.'

'What do you mean, out of it?' asks the lady, not batting an eyelid about the whole suicide thing.

'Well, she'd been upset with people at work, she'd quit—there was a legal wrangle. And now this, obviously . . .'

'So were you two very close? Is that why everyone's so concerned?'

'Well, at one point yes, I guess we were. But then we sort of drifted apart—you know, you start doing your own thing. Work becomes everything in your life. You know how the media world is.' I look at her for reassurance, a nod, a smile. I don't get anything, which I find perturbing, but I keep going.

'So you try and stay close, like make plans to hang out

every so often—and then she got this boyfriend, this older, married colleague, and uh . . . things got a little complicated.'

'How so?'

'Well, we stopped hanging out all that much . . .'

'You didn't approve of the relationship?'

'No, it wasn't that. Not like it was the healthiest, but it wasn't really that. We just stopped making plans together . . . and then, well, he hit her in public, and she didn't really stand up for herself the first time.' I stop, to just centre myself. 'She tried to the next time he did, but well, no one really cared.' I'm getting no reaction from her, it's like talking to the plants. 'I made a fuss about that at work. So my bosses are obviously aware that I was really sort of, you know, close to her.' I try to end strongly, but maybe I shouldn't have brought up the physical abuse, I realise belatedly.

'What kind of fuss?'

God, this woman is annoying me. She has this faint tone of—I can't quite put my finger on it, I think it's superciliousness. Or superiority. I think she thinks she's above all this—my stuff. Can't figure out quite what she thinks of me yet, though.

I have no choice but to go on, though. 'Well, before she actually threatened to sue them, the office, she was in a very bad way—humiliated at work. I spoke to our boss about it. I don't think it's such a big deal, but I guess that's what they might be worried about. Now that she's dead.' There, I said it.

It's so real now. She's not coming back. What a sobering thought . . . I grow quiet with that. The crap they tell you

about how the dead live on in our hearts, in our memories—
that's just for us to feel better. It's the ultimate betrayal,
death. And it doesn't matter in the least what kind of
legacy you think you're leaving behind. All that matters is
what people say about you, what they drop in conversation.

All this frikkin' lady's going to know about Rashmi is
the crap I'm telling her over some forty minutes or so.
What a depressing bloody thought.

It's hard for me to stay clear-eyed, but I guess she laps
it up, me breaking into tears at that moment. 'Sorry about
this, I'm still a bit emotional . . . I can't believe she's gone,
really.'

'No, that's fine, M. Let it out, it's okay.'

Silence.

'Do you feel guilty? Do you feel like you let Rashmi
down by not being there for her, in her new relationship?'

What the fuck?

'No,' I say quite definitively, daring her to ask me more.
Is she insane? Why the hell would I feel guilty about us
growing apart, when Rashmi made that decision to continue
seeing Susheel? She knew how I felt. And anyway, that's
not exactly how we grew apart. More like she dropped off
the face of the earth, and understandably, I suppose,
trying to deal with the aftermath of Susheel. She called
me when she was ready. And it just strikes me right there
and then, that I am in fact angry with Rashmi, for not
letting me in, for leaving me out, and leaving me behind,
then as much as now.

But I don't have the mind space or energy to tell this
complete stranger any of this.

So I let us sit there in silence.

POST-BREAKDOWN   189

'Is there anything else you want to talk about?'

'No, not really. I mean, I'm not sure why else I was asked to come to see you—do you have a file or did they tell you anything?' I'm trying desperately to get some leads here.

'That's not really how it works. I do get referrals like yourself from offices sometimes, but not often. My job is to evaluate how you're coping—what you need, that kind of thing.' She looks at me, not unkindly.

'Well, this is what I have to deal with. And my coping strategies included taking a couple days of forced leave. I went to my parents' house and took my mother with me for the last rites ceremony. I couldn't really go to that alone . . .'

'Were you close to the family?' she asks. Good question.

'Well, not that close—but I knew her brother Saad, we've all hung out. I'd met her mum over the past few years. I was pretty close to Rashmi when we first joined the channel, so yeah, they know me, I guess. It's tough on them, right now.'

Another chunk of silence.

Luckily, I think up some questions. 'Do you have any, well, advice or . . . um, experience you could share on how best to deal with this . . . mourning period?'

'Well, everyone processes their grief differently. You might want to write about it, talk to her other friends. It's just important to know that you can do that, express yourself—rather than keeping it all in.'

'True, that. Thanks, I'll figure it out,' I say, pretty lamely.

I get up, a little too abruptly. I can't think of what else

to do. 'I guess we're pretty much done here, doctor.' Except it comes out as a question. I don't really need her reassurance or anything. I just figure I've come in, had the chat and should be about done.

'Well, I do have a form for you to fill out. It's a basic, well, it's a questionnaire. I think that would be helpful. We can take it from there.'

'Oh, all right.' I take the form from her, and sit down again to go over it. Basic is right. I'm pretty sure this is a standard questionnaire to screen depression. I've seen these in magazines. I make sure to tick all the appropriate boxes. The last thing I need is for office to think that I'm a head case, you know? It strikes me that this level of paranoia about office is not entirely healthy, but I don't bring that up. Talk about laying yourself open.

All I want to do at this point is get back to work, get on with my life, and leave the meddling eyes behind me. I finish the questionnaire, hand it over to Dr Sharma and ask her what's next.

'I'll go through this and then mail a report to you and to your office. Thanks for coming in to see me. We'll see if you want to schedule anymore sessions.'

I nod and take her leave. As soon as I'm outside her office, I light up a cigarette. This last year has been hell on my lungs. That too, after a full six months of not smoking. No kidding. Well, I did smoke on and off when I was drinking—and paid the price for it, with my throat catching at awkward moments when on air. It's not for nothing that most TV people tend to take good care of their voices. Some of the hard-core ones I know only have warm drinks: no soda even, let alone cigarettes! Whatever,

POST-BREAKDOWN 191

I barely count myself as a TV person anymore, and as I tell those wanks, it's the unbelievably high air pollution in this city that will kill you, never mind a pack a day. They say it's like smoking five cigarettes a day, just living here. Might as well take ownership of that and get some satisfaction, I think, inhaling deeply.

As I stand there, I realise I'm not feeling the office vibe today. I don't feel like working at all. I text my boss to check in, and say I'll be back at work tomorrow, that I've seen the counsellor.

'Ok', he replies. Clearly he's not fond of long replies.

I get into my car and zone out . . . such a relief . . . my mind's been jumping around too much of late. And of course my parents choose that moment to call, though I don't even hear the phone ring. I see the missed calls only when I'm home. Luckily, it's not even rush hour yet, when the whole Nizamudin stretch is backed up for kilometres, so even with a quick stop-over at Khan Market en route, I get home in forty-five minutes flat.

I've gone all out: short of an IV drip of caffeine and chocolate, this is the best I can do—two slabs of imported dark chocolate and a snack pack at the cramped little store that sells everything, home-made and firang. A little pick-me-up.

With the chocolate and nicotine I'll be fine in no time. At least, that's what I'm hoping.

6. Raking in the Karma

The phone rings again as I walk into my flat.

'Hi Mum, no . . . yeah it went fine.' As always, we're both trying to talk at the same time. She's worried because I didn't pick up the phone with the first call. I give her some quip about deafening traffic.

'So what did she ask you?'

'Well, it was pretty straightforward. She wanted to know why I thought I'd been sent there, so I told her about the Rashmi thing.'

'Well, what did you tell her?'

'I told her we were close, and that Rashmi's been off for a while. Or rather had been off.' I have to get used to the past tense. 'And that she killed herself, and that of course office would be worried about the effect on me, and stuff.'

'Hmm.' She sounds non-committal.

'What? Why? You think that sounds bad? Or makes me sound bad?' I'm a little apprehensive, maybe that damn session didn't go well at all.

'No, no, I'm sure it went fine. But I'm wondering if you might have unintentionally come off sounding a little too defensive.' She's not mincing her words. I get a hollow feeling. 'But anyway, baby, if they are putting you through the grind, you need to think about whether this is what you want to be doing with your life—you could always think about other options.'

Is she saying I might have made a bad impression? I never realised how important I thought this job was till now.

'You don't think that's a little premature, Mum? Other options? I mean, I'm still good at what I do—wouldn't they at least think a little before letting me go?'

'Of course, of course,' she tries to soothe my pride. 'No doubt about that—you're the most talented young person they have there, no doubt about that. But I'm just concerned for you. If your boss thinks that Rashmi had somehow got you doing her fighting for her, god bless the poor girl, it might not be the best thing for your career.'

Doing her fighting for her?

Oh dammit . . . and I haven't even told her how I went behind Samit's back and spoke to the cops.

'I better talk to Samit when I go in tomorrow,' I tell her, mainly to get off the phone. I'm in so much shit if Samit's found out about that stunt. Really, who the fuck am I kidding, trying to play hero—or martyr. I can't afford to go down like this. It's not like I can save anyone, or save Rashmi now, or her reputation with my antics—god, why didn't I think that bloody move through.

The need for revenge is gone. All of a sudden I feel small, manipulated, from beyond the grave even. Rashmi, always getting me to fight her fights for her. Hiding behind me, when she wasn't brave enough to—oh god, I'm being a bitch now about a dead person. Really low.

Really though, it's like I'm unable to stop myself. I need a time-out.

'Mum, I'll be fine. I will. I'm always fine. Don't worry,' I tell her, a little forcefully.

'Of course you will be, baby, I know.' She's doing the mother voice again. 'You're at work right now, aren't you?'

'Well, I just . . .' How to phrase this in the most normal, least whacko kind of way? 'I thought I'd take the rest of the day off, and go in first thing tomorrow,' I say it matter-of-factly.

'But you should have just gone for a little bit, you know, just to show them what a little fighter you are,' she says. I don't think she's considered for one second that I might genuinely have some mental issue, like—I don't know— depression maybe? Her generation doesn't think depression is a real illness at all, more like a cop-out for spoiled brats who have too much money and much too much free time growing up; brats who inevitably blame their parents for everything that's wrong in their lives.

Not cluing her in is an act of kindness right now, especially. 'Yeah, well Mum, I wasn't really feeling up to it, and I told my boss that I'd be in tomorrow.'

There's a moment's silence and then, 'Well, I suppose you know what you're doing.'

I'm weary now, simply unable to cope. I need to get off the phone now. I have another call to make, see if my job's intact.

'Okay Ma, I have to give one of my colleagues a call. I'll talk to you later, okay?'

'Okay bye, baby, feel better,' she says. 'Talk soon.'

Great, more talking.

But I do have to make a couple of calls to office, and I am not looking forward to that at all, so I procrastinate a little. Wash a few dishes and put some water to boil for coffee, light up a cigarette, try to catch my breath. And stop my thoughts from running away with me.

'Okay, let's do this thing,' I say to myself. It helps to clear my head—talking to myself out loud.

First, the easier call. 'Hi Mo, this is M,' I start off, tone all chipper. 'How are things?'

'Hi!' Mohan's sounding good, no sign of strain—they haven't got to him yet, I'm thinking. 'Where have you been? I was looking for you at work today.'

'Oh, I had an appointment, something I had to do. I'll be in tomorrow, though. Why, is everything okay?'

'Yeah, but dude, haven't you heard?'

'Heard what?'

'Man, Nikhil has been going berserk all over office. I've never seen him like this. He was crying practically, couldn't go on air for one of his own specials.'

'What? Why?' This is making no sense. Nikhil? What the hell does he have to do with it?

'Well, the cops wanted to speak to Susheel. After you told them, you know, about his date and that um . . . operation Rashmi had to have.' Oh, I hope to god this young fool has not told the whole world I told the cops.

'So, they called him in for questioning, and well, he didn't show up for the appointment. No one knew where he was—his phone was off, office couldn't help, either.'

'What! You're kidding. But what does this have to do with Nikhil?'

'I'm coming to that. You won't believe this but apparently Susheel was hiding out at Nikhil's house. Apparently Susheel *didn't* tell Nikhil the cops wanted to question him.

POST-BREAKDOWN 199

Then finally when the cops finally followed up and landed up at Nikhil's house, they mistook one for the other, and brought *Nikhil* in for questioning!' His voice has an edge of excitement.

'Oh god, were they—did they—I don't know, beat him or what?'

'No no, nothing that hard-core. But they stuck him in the thana, waiting for the SHO for a few hours, just to teach him a lesson, you know, for not showing up, and all . . . But finally this whole thing was sorted out, he called us at office and we got it sorted,' he says. 'But god, by then Nikhil's wife—she was freaking out, thinking he'd done something terrible. Because he wasn't home that night, they were asking her about that scene he had with . . .' he trails off. 'And well, anyway, he's in with the big guys now, and the cops are talking to Susheel, finally.'

I'm bursting with questions, but need to play it cool. 'So anyway,' he practically shouts, 'that's why I was looking for you—I know how much you love drama around here!'

Oh, he doesn't even know the half of it.

'Listen, Mohan, you didn't . . . you didn't tell anyone else did you, that I told the cops about Susheel—it's a very delicate situation, you know?'

There's a pause. Oh god, he did, the young gossiping fool. He's gone and ruined everything. I better start thinking of some good explanations.

'Oh shut up, M. What do you think I am?' Mohan sounds indignant. 'I saw how upset you were. Of course I didn't bring your name in. In fact, if you want I can just call the cops now, and get them to remove your name from the statement.'

200 BROKEN NEWS

Now there's an idea—this is why I love the kid. Completely enterprising, independent-thinking. I feel like giving him a giant, enormous hug, if not more.

'No Mohan, I think that should be fine, just that, well, I hope they're not going to call me in for any sort of questioning . . .' I let my voice do that thing where it sort of breaks, all emotional-like. 'It's been a very traumatic experience, this whole thing, you know?'

'Of course. Don't worry, sweetie. I'll take care of it.'

'Oh thank you, Mo, you're a lifesaver—you really are.' I'm genuinely touched at how he can feel protective of me, when I'm so clearly older than him. He's a good one, this kid.

'Don't have to thank me,' his voice goes all gruff. 'I'll see you in office tomorrow—or better, let me take you out for a drink, or you know, coffee or something. I want to make sure you're okay.'

Aww, the cutie. 'Okay, it's a date, I'll see you then.'

So that did not go over half as bad as I thought. Let me put this together: Susheel has got to be in the doghouse, no matter how high his connections go, his father's hot-shot job or not—these guys at work cannot afford to fuck with the cops or interfere with a murder investigation.

That's awesome news.

Nikhil though, poor fellow, I wonder why he had to go through all this crap. I don't think he's going to be able to figure out that I helped nail Susheel, and even if he does, there's no way he can tell the bosses without implicating himself—I mean he gave me half the information I had.

So far, so good. I haven't let Rashmi down, but I haven't let myself down either. I'm not getting fired, it doesn't look like. But there is one thing I'm concerned about—and that is why Deepa hasn't bothered to call.

I call her immediately, as soon as the thought crosses my mind—there's something odd about the fact that she hasn't gotten in touch since last we spoke, even to check up on me.

'Hi Deepa, it's me. You got a second?'

'Sure, of course. Tell me, what's up?'

'Nothing, well, you know I had to go for Rashmi's cremation, I'm just . . .' my voice cracks a bit. 'Anyway, no I'm calling 'cause I have no idea what's going on at work.' I'm going to play dumb, and also pray to god this girl hasn't double-crossed me.

'Oh right, sorry, sorry I haven't called. I mean, listen, I've been so busy—they gave me your work on the series in addition to what I'm already doing—I haven't had any time to breathe . . .'

'Hey that's okay. Just wanted to check in,' I allow my voice to thaw a bit. 'Any news in office on the Rashmi thing? Or even about me?'

'I mean everyone's talking about it, obviously, but no, nothing like that—don't worry. No one's even really noticed you're gone.'

Ouch. That came out a little bitchy. 'Oh good.' But I'm surprised she hasn't heard anything. 'Did the boss say anything to you?'

'Umm, no. Well, actually, only that you might not be able to help out with the series till like later this week, so I should go ahead and take over . . . That's okay with you, right?' Something's happened. The old Deepa would have called me immediately to check if it was 'okay with me'.

202 BROKEN NEWS

I don't know what's going on, and I'm not entirely comfortable not knowing where she stands. But this is really not the time for any of this.

'Hey of course, yeah, no problem. Go for it, you're a kick-ass producer, you'll do great.' There's a fine line between being supportive and just plain ass-kissing, and dammit, I think I've crossed it. But on the whole I'm happy for her. I think. Just one tiny little part of me thinks she's used my disgrace or almost-fall from grace to her advantage, but hey, I would have done the same, right? Hell, it could've been worse news.

'Okay, well, I'll let you get back to work then, babe,' I say.

'Okay, cool. I'll see you soon. I hope you're, um, all right and stuff.' But she's not really sounding concerned. Which is a little mean, but she obviously does have a lot on her plate.

'I'm fine. I'll see you, bye,' I say, seeing no point in prolonging the conversation. She'll obviously sense my disappointment this way, but I have more serious issues to process. Like the death of my friend. Like the fact that I might have been very, very close to cracking up. That I have to get back to work tomorrow and kick some serious ass so I don't have to keep worrying about my job.

That I'm going to get that series back, if it kills me.

The next day, I'm back at work bright and early. The lady who cleans my place came and well, cleaned, which is always a good start to my day, because dust and dirt make me more neurotic than normal. I get in to work a full half-hour before anyone else on my team, so I think I should get plus points there. No idea what the

POST-BREAKDOWN   203

psychologist is going to say to the boss, though. Hopefully he'll see me at it bright and early, and that'll win him over.

That's the plan, anyway. My inbox is over-flooded and not accepting any new mails, so I have my work cut out deleting mails. And no blanket delete either—you never know when you might overlook something that could be important. And blasted Outlook, I still haven't gotten around to flagging mails from the higher-ups. Deepa, now—she's colour-coded them all, on the basis of hierarchy. Quite a clever one, that girl.

I see Samit coming in, and then heading for the meeting. I debate going, but then again, I'm feeling a little shaky. I haven't been in for a couple days, so not sure what I'd contribute.

But what about the series? As far as I can tell, I'm off the mailing list on that one—unless that's just because my inbox died on me. I can't quite put my finger on it, but I'm getting a strange feeling about the whole thing. I send Deepa an email, asking for the list of stories again. She's not in yet, it doesn't look like. Curious.

And then I see them coming out of the conference room, Deepa and Samit. She's laughing at something he's just said—you can see he's pleased, with his little moustache curling up at the end, and she, she's giving him this intent look, to reiterate a connection . . . I don't know what's changed here, but my stomach's turning.

Here I am, almost derailed completely, grieving over someone they all knew, and they just go about their everyday stuff, as if none of it matters. I don't matter, the dead girl doesn't matter . . . it's just plain inhuman . . . But you know what, it's *me* that doesn't fit. I need to get a grip.

204 · BROKEN NEWS

The news business is certainly not forgiving, that's for sure. I mean, of course they won't fire you even if you don't really fit into the master-plan—not even if you're glaringly incompetent. They'll just put you out to pasture and let you hang yourself. That's not something I want to see happening with me.

I take a look at the anchor scheds, and I'm not slotted for the next two weeks—two whole weeks. Janki, on the other hand, has every single early morning show, and a few of mine besides! It's as fast as that—meteoric rise and equally, the fall. A trifle melodramatic, I admit, but still.

I need to keep my game face on. 'Hi Deepa, Samit,' I trill, as they pass by my desk. 'How's it going?'

'Good, good . . . Good to see you back at work,' Samit says, a bit gruffly. 'You can help Deepa with some of this workload on the series—it's really a ball-buster.' They both guffaw.

'Sure thing, boss,' I say, smiling politely. 'Deepa, can I sit with you on the plan—I need the list of stories again,' I tell her, trying not to sound awkward and formal, but of course that's exactly how it comes out.

'Sure . . .' She gives me a look, incomprehensible from where I'm sitting, but whatever.

Samit leaves us to it, and I try and ease things a bit. 'So how's it going? How've you been holding up?' Technically, this is a question she should be asking moi, methinks.

'I should be asking you!' she says exactly the right thing. 'Sorry, it's been so busy and crazy around here. I was meaning to call, just . . .' she trails off. That's better though. A little bit of a thaw, I feel—a rapprochement, even.

POST-BREAKDOWN 205

Good, I'm nice right back. 'Hey, don't worry about it. I know you've been super-busy and all.' That's true enough, at my expense, I think, but don't say. 'And I'm fine, so it's all good.'

'Oh good. So the thing with, well, Rashmi, and then the counsellor—it went okay?' I can't tell whether she's genuinely concerned or just sending out feelers.

'Yeah, yeah, I mean I'm devastated obviously, but . . . and yeah, the counsellor was fine—wait, so how'd you hear about that?' I'm feeling a little embarrassed about it, even though, yes, I know there's nothing wrong with seeking help, or seeing a therapist, or anything—just that, well, of course people start talking and thinking you're deficient somehow. There is a stigma, no doubt about it.

'Oh, didn't you tell me?'

'Oh yeah, right,' I'm getting a little hazy here, so much to keep track of. 'I thought maybe word got around office too, you know how these things are.'

She looks a little green. 'Um, yeah, well, Samit may have mentioned it as well,' she says with a very guilty look on her face. I can't believe this—them gossiping about me.

'Oh yeah? What'd he say exactly?' I'm trying not to sound inquisitorial—a word that describes my tone exactly. I'm really offended, but need to stay calm, I want to give her a chance to tell me everything.

'Um, well, just that he'd asked you to, sort of, see a counsellor, and that you weren't keen, but that you . . . um . . . went . . .'

'That's true, I wasn't keen. You know, it's such a frikkin' . . . well, anyway. Did he say he'd heard how it went?'

206   BROKEN NEWS

She looks decidedly uncomfortable now. I really have to play her. 'Hey listen, Deeps, it's not on you—it's not your fault they're dealing with this whole situation, with me, and everything this way. I just want to know what he said. Where they stand.' True enough, you know. Except the part about me not blaming her for her complicity.

'Well, he just said it seemed to have gone well—he just told me this morning, in fact. And that you'd be back at work, and that . . . um . . . well, that you're well. He wasn't very polite about it—said you'd not lost it after all, that you're not nuts.'

'What a wanker! Like he gives a fuck.' I'm really pissed off now. With her as well, grease-ball—pretending to be my friend and listening to all this crap about me.

'Hey I'm sorry, but you know what he's like.' Yeah, yeah, bitch, try and put us on the same side. As if.

'Yeah, okay, well, never mind. Let's focus on this series. What's been happening with that?'

She looks relieved that I'm dropping it. The old me would have never let it go, but I'm learning where and how to pick my fights now. In my head, I know that I have to get back on top somehow, even if it kills me. And then walk the fuck out that door. Ideally, to another channel, with better pay and a better designation and more airtime. We get calls every other week, people sounding us out. Three are set to launch, two more in the pipeline—it's no joke. There's no dearth of opportunities, right here in Delhi, but the trick is to not quit when you're down and out. Because then you're desperate and get taken advantage of. Or worse than that, no return call.

I'm obviously smarter than that.

So I need to get back on top of things. I realise I've totally blanked out for the last five minutes, while this chick has been going on about the series. Got to focus here, dammit.

'And that's why it's such a huge problem with this girl, it's just unbelievable,' she's saying.

'Wait, sorry to interrupt—can I get a printout of the story ideas and then we can look at deliverables and mark the ETAs.' I'm sounding more in charge, all professional— I can feel it. The rest of the stuff I can process later.

She gets the printout and we get to work, discussing ideas, how they should be shot, which reporters are slacking off and need to be taken in hand. We split the work left between us. I decide to do one of the special stories on, well, a whim. They need to know that I can out-perform any one of their golden girls, hands down.

The day goes by this way, not half-bad and with me beginning to feel something like my earlier bustling, creative, efficient self, as does the next day. At least until I get a call that just throws me completely.

7. Shattering the Calm

It's Nikhil.

'Hey, are you okay? I wanted to call as soon as I heard, but things got way out of hand, and . . .' He trails off. I've never heard him sound this emotional. Ever.

'Yeah, I'm fine. At work, in fact. What's up?' If I didn't know me, I'd be fooled by this nonchalance thing. I think I have it down pat.

'Oh really? Oh, okay wait, I'll be there in like a half-hour, I need to talk to you. It's important,' he says, and seeing as he's never sounded like this in his entire life, I'm willing to wait for him, to chat.

Of course I imagine it has to do with me talking to the cops, even though Mohan told me no one else heard about that. Oh my god, why is my life so frikkin' complicated? I've had enough drama in the past year to last forever. If this had been years ago, it would have been fine. I was younger and hotter then, a rising star—nothing really touches you at that point, nothing can. But now, the hits, they keep coming. Just a stray comment from a random colleague can throw you.

'Hey, how's it going? Heard about the mess—I feel so bad for you,' says Mallika, she of the city team. Slightly

212 BROKEN NEWS

bitchy girl, but has always been nice to me even though she was angling for an anchor slot, which didn't work out.

'I'm okay, thanks.' My standard reply.

'Oh god, it's just terrible—so much stress . . .' she says, sounding like she actually cares.

'Yeah, well, it's not just that . . . Rashmi's death—it's bigger than any of this work stuff,' I say, quite sincerely. These bastards are acting like it hasn't happened—that someone we knew and worked with, and most of us liked, killed herself, driven to the worst point of desperation.

'Yeah, I know, that really sucks. It's terrible. But for you also . . .'

'She was my friend, so . . .' I shrug. I'm not sure where this conversation is leading, but obviously there's a point.

Then she goes straight for the jugular. 'Poor you, I feel terrible, I mean, you look like death . . . and I do that too, eat a lot when I'm stressed, it's showing a bit though, darling, tch-tch,' she clicks her tongue. 'They should let you take some time off,' is her final barb, as she saunters off.

The skinny bitch. It's un-fucking-believable, all these insects waiting to take a swipe at you. They don't have the balls to try it until you're down and bloody out.

The problem is, it works too. I run to the bathroom, and spend the next ten minutes looking at myself in the mirror. I never used to buy into this shit. Five years ago, I did the whole ranting and railing against the status quo, against the way women are made to feel. But as I stare myself down in the mirror, I know I've sold out. I've done the gamut: fasting, purging, bingeing, trying to package myself, sell myself, trying to sex-up my profile . . . *this* is the level I'm sinking to, to keep my job?

POST-BREAKDOWN 213

No need to get sanctimonious though—this *is* my job, I tell myself.

Luckily something comes along to take the attention away from me: Nikhil. He calls on my cell, just as I'm exiting the bathroom, ready to slit my wrists for what I've done to myself. And to think I was top of my graduating class in college—hoping to change the world.

Nikhil meets me downstairs at the little café. I'm getting my cappuccino straight up, hoping the caffeine will perk me up. He looks—well, stricken—there's no other word for it. I've never seen Captain Stylish with a hair out of place, ever. That's who he's been since college.

And yet today, his shirt's all rumpled, his eyes are bloodshot and he might even have that dirty stubble thing going—very sexy on some people, no doubt, just not a regular Nikhil look.

'Hey man, what's going on? Are you okay?' I give him a hug before sitting down—he's really looking down and out.

'I'm fine . . . I mean, I'm not. I need to talk to you about something important,' he says, and he does not sound his usual self at all. 'But first, I wanted to ask you how it's going? I mean, they weren't really expecting you back, were they?'

'Why on earth not? Where'd you get that from?'

'Oh M . . . no one. I just heard, y'know? I think they thought you'd take some time off, because of Rashmi. God knows I would have . . . especially after the cops—' he stops.

'The cops what?' My heart stops, I swear to god. Samit is going to fire my ass. I didn't think he knew that I'd spoken to the goddamn cops.

214 BROKEN NEWS

'Oh, they wanted to talk to you, didn't they get in touch?' He sounds quizzical.

I have no idea what to say. Maybe it doesn't matter because it *is* Nikhil. But I better get my story straight, in case Samit asks me. I grab my phone to text Mohan—he'll find out what the cops said to management. I just shake my head at Nikhil; he's still staring at me. 'Maybe because my phone's been off for the last couple of days,' I say.

He looks puzzled, but doesn't push it. 'Anyway, I wanted to talk to you about something else. Something about Rashmi,' he starts, and stops as the guy comes to give us our coffee. 'I don't know, she might have mentioned it to you?'

'Nikhil, stop being so damn cryptic, get to the point. I have no idea what you're talking about.' Talking about Rashmi to the flake of all flakes is making me a little jittery, I admit.

'God, I can't believe she didn't tell you,' he stops to take a huge swig of coffee. I'm thinking a drink would do him more good, at this point. 'Anyway, someone told the cops, and they brought it up—so I don't know whether anyone in office knows . . .' He's not making any sense yet, but I don't want to stress him out further by asking for coherent sentences.

'The thing is, I need you to find out what people know, you know? It's bloody important. It's just that I can't get over—it was just the one time and —'

He's not making sense—and then in one bloody second it becomes clear, and the pit in my stomach turns to ice.

'It's that I didn't know . . . I don't know who else to talk to, M,' he says imploringly. 'I don't know who else to trust.' The shallow twit is mouthing all these inanities. I don't think he ever figured his Casanova gig would catch up with him. He's always been way too smooth for that. 'I slept with her the *one* time,' he's explaining. 'She'd called me about the Susheel heartbreak. And we went out, had a couple of drinks ... you know how she gets, how she used to get,' he corrects himself, and yes of course I remember how she used to get: from hard-ass to marshmallow in an instant, and it didn't take much for guys to have their way with her. Though I know she used to act a little drunker than she was; it was the sex, and the full freedom from liability courtesy the booze, that she milked.

'So what's the deal, why are you telling me this now? Did Rashmi call you before she died or what?'

'No, no, it came out ... the cops were questioning Susheel about the fact that—I don't know if you knew— she was pregnant.' He looks at me out of the corner of his eye. I give nothing away.

'Pregnant?' I ask, instinctively going for ignorance, my head reeling. Why on earth had I immediately assumed it was Susheel? Why? When the truth is that my friend Nikhil, the one we keep making excuses for year after year, because his looks and charm and charisma can blind you to his moral lassitude.

I was on the warpath when it came to Susheel, Samit was right about that part. And the whole time, this weasel, my friend the dirt-bag, was the one to blame: knocking women up and wriggling out of responsibility and letting them kill themselves.

It's obscene not just because it's *him*, but because I'm

clearly just as fat-headed and judgemental and biased as the rest of them. How the hell did I get so bloody self-righteous?

'What the fuck is wrong with you?' I ask him. 'Didn't you fucking use protection? I mean, come on Nikhil, you do this often enough, you should be smarter than that.'

'I know, I know.' His voice is small, but I think he enjoys being castigated. It probably makes the guilt somehow easier to bear. 'I should have, but we got carried away. I can barely remember what happened that night, I was so hammered.' Ah, alcohol as a get-out-of-jail-free card—it's uncanny how often it's used.

'Anyway, someone told the cops—I don't know who— I guess someone from office, that she'd had an abortion. They came for Susheel, to interrogate him, and he was at my place—what a mess, his wife hasn't even spoken to him since then.' He stops and starts up again, oblivious to my silence.

'Anyway, Rashmi and Susheel, they were trying to re-ignite things. They'd been seeing each other again a while, but not long—like a few weeks, max. And then this. She wanted to have this baby with him, and god knows, he wasn't going to leave his wife. He told her to get an abortion,' Nikhil pauses as he works out what happened. 'I guess she did it and after that, somehow, he figured it wasn't his baby.' Nikhil looks nervous now. Susheel can be scary.

'She told him about me. And he got furious. He . . .' Nikhil's voice trails off again. 'He got abusive, he yelled at her. Called her a dirty whore, the bartender told the cops. He just left, ended it, and then she . . . she killed herself.'

POST-BREAKDOWN 217

Why the hell didn't she call *me*? I think. I would have helped her. Except—the last conversation we had, I was so ready to defend her against the unseen, I was attacking Susheel, wasn't I. My blind prejudice would've gotten in the way of her telling me anything.

God, I feel like such a fucking failure.

But I still need to figure out exactly what happened. 'But then why the fuck would Susheel stay with you, Nikhil? He must've been furious?'

Nikhil just shakes his head. 'Shall we go out for a smoke?' he tries.

'No, we won't go out for a smoke, Nikhil, this is fucking serious,' I snarl at him, and then I realise, they both decided to cover for each other. Neither of them looking good in this bloody mess. 'Of course he did confront you, didn't he . . . so you tried to cover for him, let him stay at yours, right? In exchange for him *not* telling anyone in office that you knocked her up?'

He nods, and doesn't even have the good grace to look ashamed.

'God, Nikhil, all you fucking care about is your own slimy bloody hide.' I'm so appalled by his behaviour, I don't know what's worse. My judgement's shot to bits. I've been so tied up trying to nail Susheel, that . . .

'M, I need your help, I wouldn't ask if I didn't have to,' he's whining now, pleading with me, on the basis of what? Just the fact that we go back longer than other people?

'I need to know if people in office know anything about this, M. It'll be really bad if this gets out, but since the cops know it—not that they think I'm a suspect or anything—but it would just be really bad.'

218 BROKEN NEWS

Of course it would, it would spoil his entire shiny super-lover image to have this little thing mar it—this inadvertently causing the derailment and death of another human being. The horror is that he doesn't care about what he's done, so much as what people say.

And they send *me* to the damn counsellor.

'It's disgusting, what you've done. Unforgivable.' I know he doesn't care, but I have to say it.

'Does Ruchi know?'

'Of course not,' he scoffs. 'She thinks it's just routine questioning to do with the . . . the death.' He looks down. 'Listen, even Preeti doesn't know. Please, M. I feel bad enough already. I haven't been able to sleep or eat or . . .'

I believe him too, but it's not enough. I just want him out of my face. 'I'll tell you what I hear,' I tell him.

And that's when I realise it. Crystal-clear. I can't stay here, I can't be part of this racket anymore. It's indecent that I'm here even now. My drive, my desire to get back my glory, it's all gone—that ambition reeks of rottenness now, of carrion. I just need a couple more answers, to set the record straight, and then I can get the hell out.

If I don't, I'm done for. I won't be able to breathe.

I push the chair back, get up to leave.

8. *Exit Point*

I get back to my desk, go through the motions of working the rest of the day. Any idiot could do this desk stuff in their sleep: whatever they tell you when you join, it's not difficult at all. To be good at it, now that's another thing—but I've just found that the price, it's too bloody high. I reply to some mails on autopilot, steer a couple of reporters in the right direction, fix up a shoot for myself for the next day. I plan to honour all my commitments before bowing out of this bizarre race altogether.

Bastards, and yet as I say it, the rage has already started to die down, leaving a cold not-quite numbness in its wake. I'm always so eager to blame someone else, sitting on my high horse. But no one actually forces you to sell out. It's a battle you fight every day, until one day you just forget, and get sucked into this artificial world with its misplaced emphases, twisted priorities. I've traded on my principles—there's no coming back from that, I can't just snap back and 'un-get' it.

It's about an hour or so before I call Mohan. 'Hey man, are you around?'

'Yup, yup! Just got back from a shoot,' he says. I just saw him a few hours ago, doing lives on TV, but you'd never know, from the way he behaves, that he's on the day's biggest story.

'So I wanted to meet you real quick, are you on your side?' I ask.

'Yeah, but give me, like, five minutes, and we can go down and grab a coffee or a quick bite.'

'Sure thing, see you.'

I pack up for the day, say bye to Deepa, tell her I'm working a story the next day. She seems fine, distant, but I'm beyond caring now. If it's this superficial, our relationship isn't worth half as much as I used to think.

I can't stomach more coffee, so I just refill my bottle with some water out of the cooler.

'Hey, how are you?' Mohan comes up and commandeers me to one of the comfier looking chairs.

'Not so bad,' I answer, half-truthfully. 'It's been a lot to deal with, obviously.'

'Of course, poor thing. Tell me, what can I do?' He's an eager one, and obviously looks up to me, at some level. I must make sure not to get him in trouble or let him down. Relationships are so fragile.

'I just wanted to check, Mo, what are they saying about the Rashmi case around office?'

He looks embarrassed. 'Well . . . actually, you know out here they're saying you'd gone and cracked up or some shit, thinking there's some sort of conspiracy involving the higher-ups.' He's certainly not one to mince words, but at least his tone is still friendly. 'But I've been shutting those rumours up wherever I hear them,' he says.

'Hey, you don't have to do that,' I say, patting him on the shoulder. 'Really. I don't want you to get in trouble on my account.' He smiles back at me. 'Truth is, I *have* been blaming office ever since she was let go, really, but whatever. I'm not going to fight them on this supposed crazy breakdown thing or whatever.'

'Well, they think you're on some crazy vendetta out to nail Susheel. He's been telling people himself, I think—I overheard someone say that,' Mohan clarifies. 'I don't know him so I'm not sure, but I know he was talking to your boss about you —'

'Did he know about what I told the cops, do you think?' It's almost of academic interest to me now, how does it even matter. Even if he was there right before Rashmi killed herself, it wasn't his baby; he's probably managed to talk his way out of this.

'Well, I'm not sure—I guess not. I mean, someone would have said something to you. No one heard it from me either, you know?' he's quick to point out.

I acknowledge that. 'Thanks man, you're the best. So have you heard any other developments on the case from the cops?'

'Yeah, but you're not going to like it, I'm afraid.' He's being brutally honest. 'It's your friend Nikhil.'

'What? What about him?'

'Well, they're saying—the cops are saying—I'm sorry, it seems he got Rashmi pregnant. It's not just that . . .' he breaks off, looking to see if I'm okay. I nod at him to go on, I don't trust myself to speak just yet. 'Susheel also knows about the whole thing, it turns out. I heard Susheel was telling Samit and the other bosses.' He pauses. Reaches out to hold my hand. 'They're looking to let him go, or at least suspend him till this thing dies down.'

224 BROKEN NEWS

I let him go on holding my hand while I try to process this. Susheel is not the guilty party here. It's Nikhil. I guess because of Rashmi's former legal case, her approaching the NCW at one point, it's potentially something that could explode, other channels were sniffing around it. But even though no one inside the media takes on one of their own, I suppose office has to take some sort of action.

'So. They're going to go after Nikhil. Susheel's off the hook? Even in terms of the police investigation?'

'Well, they've questioned him obviously. He explained he wasn't avoiding them, just in shock, and depression, so they haven't been too hard on him.'

I roll my eyes. Typical. 'What about the argument they were having the night she killed herself?' I ask.

'Well, he's told them he ended things with Rashmi long back, but that she was unstable. The cops figure he had nothing to do with her suicide per se. They're saying, off the record, it was Nikhil's fault—if anyone's—that Rashmi and Susheel were even fighting at the bar that night.

'I'm sorry, I know this is hard for you,' he tells me, eyes softening. I just wait for him to pick up the story, so I can be done with all this. 'They did check back with Rashmi's family, who are still devastated, obviously. They don't want anything to do with this, so for the cops it's pretty much case closed, you know?'

So somehow Susheel outplayed them all. He outplayed her and he damn well outplayed Nikhil. He's getting off fucking scot-free—no one thinks he has anything to do with Rashmi's death. What do you pin him with? Breaking up with her? Someone the world considered unstable in any case, thanks to him? He's lied through his teeth to the cops, I'm sure, just as he's done with his wife, like he did to Rashmi, holding out the promise of divorce. And she fell for it, the one-time hard-ass cynic. Poor darling girl.

'I have very little sympathy for Nikhil,' I tell Mohan, just so he knows. I don't add that I think Nikhil's really been out-manoeuvred. 'I don't feel that bad for him, to be honest, because with all his dicking around, I think he's been asking for trouble for a long time,' I continue. Whether he should be fired—god only knows. Would that serve any purpose? I suppose not.

As for me, I decide I've had enough. I give Mohan a hug, thank him for all his help.

I walk back up, log back on to my machine, click on New Message and To all: Samit, the anchor-in-charge, the big boss. This is very bad exit strategy: you're supposed to give them some warning, the people you work for. But I'm tapped out.

And they don't deserve the slightest courtesy from me, that's for sure. I hope I don't regret this, a little voice tells me, but I ignore it. I can't see through the blanket of red.

Hi,

It's been a privilege to work for you till now. Unfortunately, unavoidable circumstances have arisen and I feel I would be untrue to myself and to you if I continued, despite them.

It has been a difficult time, with Rashmi's death marring what has otherwise been a great work experience.

I will serve my one month's notice.

Thanks,

M.

226 BROKEN NEWS

I hit Send.

And walk out the building.

I sleep really well that night, an alcohol-induced haze; Ankita and Karthik take my SOS call, come over to mourn with me. They've been wanting to reach me for days, it turns out, but didn't want to intrude.

'Intrude in my space, please,' I tell them. 'Please.'

And I'm crying, even as they tell me I'm doing the right thing, regaining my integrity, that they'll help me look for a job. We drink and smoke and I feel not-alone. Rashmi's suicide jarred us all—it touched everyone she knew, because it just went to show how close we are to the edge, at any given time.

Any fucking time, you could lose just about anyone you care about.

Yourself, even.

I wake up the next morning, mildly hungover, but ready to face up to the enormity of the day at work.

My phone rings a couple of times in the morning— it's Samit calling, saying to meet him when I get in to work. Ominously, that's the only call, considering how back in the day my phone was guaranteed to go off three or four times by 9.30 a.m.

I get into work, and log on. Nothing spectacularly different happened as I walked in the door, but without a shade of a doubt I know that every single person in that room—from the fifteen-odd desk jockeys to the five or so video editors milling around, to the guys in the small cabins by the back—every single person knows I've quit.

They also know the contents of the reply to my email, before I do. I don't know quite what I'm expecting, but here's what I get.

POST-BREAKDOWN 227

The super-boss writes:

Dear M,

I'm sorry to hear that you will be leaving us. But I do wish you all the best in your journey onward.

Best, X.

Before I get a chance to meet Samit, his email (marked to all) pops in my inbox:

M, I'm sorry that you're leaving us, but am confident that you will excel wherever you go. HR to pl note leaving period can be suspended in this case. Consider contractual obligations fulfilled. All best.

No reply from the anchor boss, but that's okay— he's been out of station, and would probably only see this on the way back.

Samit's mail takes a while to sink in. Not only are they not angling to keep me—a standard work procedure, where they give you an emotionally-loaded speech and incentives to stay on—they're not even making me serve my notice period. Which means I don't even need to be here today.

They're more than happy that I'm getting out. It's like they'd already decided—my brain fog clears. They would basically have hounded me into oblivion, till I'd literally have been forced to leave—that's the way they roll. There's no place here for my sort. Their loss, I try and tell myself, game face on. But I'm really feeling low now.

I walk over to Samit's cabin, but he's not there. I text him saying I'll come meet him when he's free.

'What the hell is going on?' Deepa comes up to me. 'What the hell are you thinking?'

'Hi Deepa, good morning to you too.' I try to be flip, but it really doesn't play.

228 BROKEN NEWS

'Why the hell are you sabotaging your own career, M, what has gotten into you?'

'Oh, I take it you heard about the mail ... it's okay Deeps, don't worry. I mean —'

'Do you even fucking know what you've done, or is this one of those things you do all spontaneously, living in your la-la land, no clue of what's going on. Your bloody career should be —'

'Oh, come off it—what bloody career? Deepa, you and I both know I've been sidelined here for a while. They're not comfortable with people who speak their own minds, they don't fucking want any independent thought—and that's fine. I'm just not playing that game anymore.'

'Oh, don't try and portray yourself as a goddamn martyr. Jesus, you've just wimped out, scared, you can't handle it anymore.' She's really angry. 'Real life, real politics—you just wimped the fuck out. I can't believe it.'

'Well, I'm sorry you feel that way. I'm sorry you can't see why I had to "wimp the fuck out"—I can't win. Not here,' I try and explain. 'I'm losing my mind. My friend went and offed herself, and the guy most responsible for it can't be held accountable, in fact he'll probably get bumped up to a prime-time show. I don't know what you're expecting me to do.'

'At the very least, show *some* sign of maturity, some sign of thinking things through. I've been waiting around for weeks for you to talk to me, let me know what's been going on—nothing. Can't get through to you on *any* level—'

'Oh come on, you could've gotten through to me if you ever gave a shit, don't give me that—and you'll make off

POST-BREAKDOWN 229

with a better deal than ever before, now that I'm out, don't worry. And I'm sorry if I've been off—my friend just died. It's not that much of a stretch for me to be down and out.'

'I can't believe you're being such a bitch,' she starts off, and calms herself down. 'Of course I understand how hard it's been,' she says in a much kinder tone. 'But the way you're reacting, acting in such haste—you've given them the perfect opportunity. I can't believe you didn't stand up and fight back. You of all people.' It's shocking—she's close to tears, practically.

I take her downstairs. I've had just about enough of being the freak-show tamasha.

'Deeps, you can't know what it's like—they haven't told the entire office you're insane, you're not getting strange looks from people . . . no one else is standing up . . .' I start off, and it's true—that's one side of it.

But this is my job, I want to say, this is my *life*, I don't know what else to do. 'But you know, that's not even the point. It would do me irreparable damage to stay here. Of course I wanted to stick it out—to fight back, as you put it. But they'll do me in, like they did Rashmi. I'm more than that. I'm not going to let myself be exploited and insulted and debased by this bullshit company.' By this time, I'm running out of conviction, almost, but I have to talk it through.

'But, M, they're going to end up ruining your life . . . where will you get a job? They won't give you references, after this.' She's genuinely concerned. It's touching. Really. Even if it's a bit late.

And of course, Deepa being Deepa, she's forcing me to some level of pragmatism.

'Oh, they will goddamn give me references, I have enough work behind me here that they can't not. I am a bloody good journalist,' I say indignantly, and she almost laughs. 'But Deeps, even if you told me with a hundred per cent certainty I wouldn't get another job in the media after this, I'd do the same thing over again.'

I've almost convinced myself. I think deep down somewhere, I was half-expecting the company to cajole me into taking back my resignation letter, into staying. Ever the sell-out, I probably would've caved. Of course I'm not sure what the hell I'm doing—I'm scared even. But it's okay, I'll deal, that much I know.

'Well. I don't know what to say to you. It's a losing battle,' says Deepa, looking dejected.

'Listen, it's not all bad. I'm going to have more time to hang out and stuff, so whenever you're bored with work and just want to shoot the shit like the old days, you give me a call.'

I get up to collect my stuff. 'I'm not even going to say bye. I know I'll see you again.'

Truth is, apart from Samit, I'm not going to say bye to anyone else anyway. Just going to delete my emails, transfer whatever files I have onto my pen drive—oh and I am so going to need a show reel at some point, a copy of clips from all the big stuff I've done.

Just not today. I'll have to come back in at some point. When it's less raw.

Samit's not going to be in, he texts me to say.

'*Okay, well boss, I guess I won't be coming in tomorrow,*' I text back. '*Thanks for everything.*'

Everything, right—especially for being a spineless bastard, I feel like adding.

POST-BREAKDOWN 231

He actually calls back. 'M,' he starts.

'Yes boss.'

'Listen, I am very . . .' he's hunting for the word, 'I'm very sorry you feel you have to go. I think you must look at this as a break.' He pauses.

'Sir, I'm not sure—' but he cuts me off.

'M, take the break, take time off, travel, relax, mourn, and then when you're done trying whatever else is out there, call me, and we'll see about coming back, okay?' He sounds way too confident that I'll even want to come back.

'I'm not sure.' I'm trying to tell him I don't think that's even a remote possibility, but he's cutting me off again.

'You take your time, you'll figure it out,' he says. 'And M, good luck.'

That's it, I'm dismissed. But it's actually the closest he's come to being nice in a long while.

'Thanks, Samit,' I say and we hang up.

I get HR on the phone to figure out about the notice period.

'Don't worry about it. Your salary's being adjusted, and we're not fining you—no notice period, Samit has told us, so . . .'

'I see.'

'Any other questions at this time?'

'No.'

'Okay, good luck, M, have a nice day now.'

Have a nice day! I'm out of a job, hardly any money in the bank, no idea where I'm going . . . You too, I mutter in my head.

I walk out, bag and heart heavier, leaving my youth and idealism behind me.

Wish Fulfilment Fantasy

I toss, I turn, I get up, bug-eyed, sleepless, furious. I don't know where I get it, but I know I have a shotgun and I know I have the balls to do this. I'm ready, I have all this rage and it's fuelling me, and I'm headed straight to the bastard's house to nail his ass, shoot him dead, and fuck what happens to me. I don't care about that, it's the revenge I'm looking for and the chance to smash this worm once and for all.

I get there, it's Nikhil . . . Nikhil who looks at me all funny as I blow a hole through his chest, not even registering my 'hello asshole', as he takes a slug not meant for him, but why the hell not, he's ruined enough lives I'm sure, slimy shit-head, supposed friend of mine, and it's Susheel I'm looking for in the back room, his eyes wide in his ugly fucking head, and I'm spraying the place, going fucking wild.

I'm awake in a second, heart racing, sweat pouring off me, and thank god, because who the hell would've got me off that one, and I don't want to end up in Tihar thank you very much, for the rest of my natural life.

But I'm sad too, in a way, because I know there's nothing I can do to make this right—whatever's happened has happened, and it's us, the little people, who really have no say in how things are run.

Epilogue

If only things were that simple. To be honest, I have to tell you that after a couple of weeks, I couldn't quite place my finger on why I was so angry with my office. Who I was really angry with, my new therapist helped me realise, was of course myself. And Rashmi.

I paid 1600 bucks for that moment of clarity.

I finally took time to do my own out-reach programme—I bonded with my parents, with friends I'd lost along the way. I went and found my ex-roomie Nisha to check up on her, tell her that I cared, to show her she's not alone. She was more than happy to see me, but showed me she of all people is really not alone. She goes to her regular AA meetings, she has friends now, she volunteers at the rehab centre—she's leading a full life.

For three weeks, I helped her out at the rehab. It's quite down-market, as we would say in TV, and that's fine with me. I'm not the snob I used to be, after all that's happened.

The circle is smaller than we think—her new best friend is my old hero, Priya. Who's more than pleased to see that I'm not the starry-eyed girl buying into the myth and magic and glitter that is television.

I went for a couple of AA meetings with Nisha, for

support—I think I needed it more than her.

One day at a time, they teach me.

One day at a time.

It's the closest I've come to being zen in ten years.

And then, I get two mails. It's like Samit said—you never *can* quite take yourself out of the circus.

There's a mail from my chat buddy Neville.

I heard what happened, I'm really sorry you've gone through such a tough time. Let me know if you want to get that drink, ever! Oh and M, there are job opportunities just waiting for you to pick and choose, all across the media, X Nev

We had our first moment—I called Neville and made a date, finally. To take this out of the virtual, into the real world—a place I need to get used to.

And a charming mail from Janki—who I've noticed has taken over my prime-time show—is what jump-starts my ego.

Hi, I just wanted to say a big hello and hope you are well. Thanks for everything, Janki.

Deep down inside, I realise part of me misses that buzz of the news, even that feeling of importance. It's just that I'd let all of that blinker me—it shut out the rest of my life. But that's not TV's fault, says that little voice in my head. I'll be calling Samit for an appointment next week.

My name is Meera, and I know that's the name in a little box on a roster somewhere . . . exactly where it belongs.

Acknowledgements

Here's where I finally get to make my Oscar-style thank you speech, clutching a statuette, blinking in the bright lights—thanks to my fave girls in all the world, Tinky and Anju, the solidest base anyone could ask for.

To the young ray of sunshine, the now altogether-grown up Bugs, words can't express!

AR, l&l, even with the uncertainty.

Pea and Moon, together my touchstone.

My girls across the world, Gerry, Ira and Shoili, for every conceivable support and incredible far-ranging conversations.

Soul sista Nemo, Oz for the spark of an idea mid-conversation, and Shiv, for dragging me out from under my rock way back when.

Meera for your namesake, Shalini for all the years in between, and your darling's name variation, and Nandini for that hilarious bountiful cow convo!

The best 'office friends' ever . . . Vanita and Seemi, been there, seen it all.

And it would be remiss not to thank teachers who helped me find my voice—the Giffords, Veronique, Mr Cousins, Eric Hillebrand, Cassandra Price, Joni Brill;

236 ACKNOWLEDGEMENTS

in boarding school, Mrs Shukla, Mrs Chopra and Mrs Dutta.

My philosophy professors, an institution in themselves, in the nicest way possible—Dr Shankaran, Dr Tankha and Mr Nanda—for all the ideas, and discussion, and the gift of philosophy.

This book isn't about *my* job or work and I have to say, I've been really lucky to have the best bosses, who saw past hesitation to the potential—even as a lowly trainee sub-editor.

Raj, thank you for handling the existential angst and going way above and beyond.

Pam for taking all my 'Time-outs' and telling me to write.

Ritu and Sagarika, for the coffee and conversation, and a great gig of a job.

Thanks also to Shekhar and Rajdeep, for all the encouragement along the way.

My editor, Deepthi Talwar, for the first commission of a writing project and staying calm through all the transformations, and Renuka Chatterjee for taking an interest!

Thanks and love to the parentals and grandparents, though I really hope they ignore all the swearing (sorry mom!!).

A shout-out to all my tweepies, feedback's welcome @amritat on twitter.